...hard oprea

TRILOGY
of
THEOPHIL MAGUS
The Truth

2008

BIO-BIBLIOGRAPHY

LEONARD OPREA (b. December 1953) is a contemporary Romanian writer.

He was born in Prejmer, a village in Braşov (Kronstadt) County in the eastern part of Transylvania, central Romania. A graduate of the University of Braşov, he specialized in mass-media communication at the University of California at Chico in 1990.

Since 1999 he has been living in the USA, currently in Auburn, Maine.

Leonard Oprea was an anti-communist dissident in Romania during Ceausescu's dictatorship. Between 1980 and 1987 he published one book and some short stories in the most important literary reviews and won many national literary prizes. After 1987 the Securitate, the secret police of the Communist regime, officially forbade the publication of his writings, considering them subversive.

After the Romanian Revolution of 1989, living in Bucharest, he became a well-known Romanian writer, journalist and editor. He was able to resume publishing his works: novels, short stories, tales and essays, meditations etc. He founded the Romanian Publishing House *Athena*, the Vladimir Colin Romanian Cultural Foundation as well as the *Vladimir Colin* international awards.

Links:

www.google.com, www.amazon.com, www.barnes&noble.com

Works:

- **Domenii interzise (Forbidden areas)** short stories and novellas; Albatros Publishing House – 1984, Romania.

- **Radiografia clipei (The X-ray of an instant)** short stories and novellas forbidden by the Romanian Communist dictatorship in 1987; Dacia Publishing House – 1990, Romania; the second edition with critical references at Curtea Veche Publishing – 2003, Romania; electronic book by "LiterNet" www.liternet.ro/, 2005, Romania.

- **Cămaşa de forţă (The Straitjacket)** a novel banned by the Romanian Communist dictatorship in 1988; Nemira Publishing

House – 1992, Romania; the second edition with critical references at Curtea Veche Publishing – 2004, Romania; electronic book by "LiterNet" www.liternet.ro/, 2005, Romania.

- **The Trilogy of Theophil Magus** – a sui-generis novel:

  o **Cele Nouă Invăţături ale lui Theophil Magus despre Magia Transilvană (The Nine Teachings of Theophil Magus on Transylvanian Magic)** – Polirom Publishing House – 2000, Romania; electronic book by "LiterNet" www.liternet.ro/, 2003, Romania.

  o **The Book Of Theophil Magus Or 40 Tales About Man (Cartea lui Theophil Magus sau 40 de Poveşti despre Om)** – Polirom Publishing House – 2001, Romania. *English version*, October 2003, edited in the USA by Ingram Book Group/ 1stBooks Library; new edition by AuthorHouse – 2004, USA; electronic book by "LiterNet" www.liternet.ro/, 2006, Romania.

  o **Meditaţiile lui Theophil Magus sau Simple Cugetări Creştine la Începutul Mileniului III (The Meditations of Theophil Magus or Simple Christian Thoughts at the Beginning of the Third Millennium)** – Polirom Publishing House – 2002, Romania; electronic book by "LiterNet" www.liternet.ro/, 2004, Romania.

- **Theophil Magus – Confessions 2004-2006** ("Universal Dalsi" Publishing House, 2007, Romania)

- **Theophil Magus in Baton Rouge – a haiku novel** ("Xlibris"/ Random House Ventures, 2008, USA)

Quotations:

In Romania, Leonard Oprea is a distinguished writer. In my opinion, here in the USA, Leonard Oprea could make a *genuine contribution* to our current writing landscape. His narrative of his immigrant experience is felicitously captured in his *novel in haiku*.
(**Andrei Codrescu** – *poet, author, NPR commentator*)

***

Theophil Magus in Baton Rouge, to the best of my knowledge, *the first novel* made up of *haiku*. In many respects it is reminiscent of the most

amazing Central European stylistic virtuosi, and I am sure readers will be delighted to enter this universe of shining plasticity.
(**Vladimir Tismaneanu** – *philosopher, author, essayist*)
***

First, there's no such thing as a *haiku novel*. At least, *not until* you've read this book. *Not until Leonard Oprea thought it could exist.* How can anyone think of hailing Jesus in a Japanese poem? In *the small* space of Leonard's *haiku novel*, you'll be taking *a giant leap of fancy*. His haiku will envelop you in its grace and will open a magic world, making you dream once again like a child.
(**Bogdan Stefanescu** – *author, essayist, literary translator*)
***

In *Trilogy of Theophil Magus' 40 Tales about Man*, a great variety of sacred and profane themes, archaic, mythical, contemporary (Moses, Gandhi, Christmas, children, journalism, pilgrimage etc.) serves as vivid stimulation for this literary adventure, written with humor, knowledge and wit . . . in an inviting dialogue with the reader.
(**Norman Manea** – novelist, essayist)
***

The Truth, the second book of *Trilogy of Theophil Magus* is situated in the strange no man's land where everyday life becomes truly magical. I consider these writings as splendid expressions of a unique vision of our fragmented but marvelously exciting world. Leonard Oprea's style combines a discovery of hidden meanings of words with a fabulous sense of secret humor. His works received the highest praises from the most influential critics, who rightly compared his vision to works by Thomas Mann, Borges or Paulo Coelho.
(**Vladimir Tismăneanu** – philosopher, author, essayist)
***

Leonard Oprea's *40 Tales* of *Trilogy of Theophil Magus – The Truth*, range from the depiction of the everyday to the mythological and Borgesian to the religious. Honored with numbers of prizes in his native Romania, this writer is a true iconoclast and a true talent.
(Adam J.Sorkin – author, essayist, editor)
***

Yes, Leonard Oprea knows how to tell his *40 Tales about Man of Theophil Magus* and all the tales of the world because he uses *la modification* to place his unmistakable fingerprint on each of them. In this, no doubt that Leonard Oprea is a genius "thief" who strangely wants to enlarge the public domain he furtively relishes, not diminish it. I repeatedly asked myself if one can say about a writer who is still alive, whom I had the privilege of knowing, that he is a very good writer, even a great one. I have always had my doubts about it until now – when I braced up and concluded that you can.
(**Liviu Antonesei** – poet, novelist, essayist)

leonard oprea

TRILOGY of THEOPHIL MAGUS
The Truth

***

The Book of Theophil Magus
or
40 Tales about Man

***

English version by Bogdan Stefanescu

***

Revised and complete edition

Cover creation by Leonard Oprea
***
Front cover – "Doubting of St Thomas" by Caravaggio about 1600,
Oil on canvas, 107 x 146 cm
***
Interior illustrations – drawings by Leonardo da Vinci (1452-1519)
***
Xlibris Editor – Steve Lundblade
Editorial adviser – Frieda Lovett
***
This book was printed in the United States of America.
***

To order additional copies of this book, contact:
Xlibris Corporation
1-888-795-4274
www.Xlibris.com
Orders@Xlibris.com
46156

CONTENTS

CHAPTER 4

CHAPTER 5

CHAPTER 6

CHAPTER 7

CHAPTER 8

AFTERWORD

These tales I dedicate to:

Anna-Maria, Brigitte, Nardviana, Milica

and

to our Angels Ara and Herta.

***

I have to thank very much Volo and Liviu who trusted in me.

Everyone has his/her own tale in here.

***

Special thanks to my translator, Bogdan Stefanescu.

A GENUINELY DIFFERENT VOICE

by *Vladimir Tismaneanu*

Leonard Oprea, a brilliant Romanian writer, the author of important fiction and non-fiction works, is one of the finest, truly original contemporary East European writers.

I have known him personally since 1990, but I had read his works long before that. Let me emphasize that Leonard Oprea, as an anti-Communist dissident played an important role in the oppositional culture during Nicolae Ceausescu's dictatorship, in Romania. Although widely known as a brilliant fiction writer, his works were censored and eventually banned in the late 1980s. He was involved in the underground anti-dictatorship activities and consequently suffered continuous police harassments.

His outstanding works of fiction, among which the poignant novel *Camasa de forta* (*The Straitjacket*) and an acclaimed volume of short stories *Radiografia Clipei* (*The X-Ray of an Instant*) were banned by the dictatorship's censors and came out only after the anti-Communist revolution in December 1989. Leonard

Oprea's books received the highest praise from the most influential critics in Romania who rightly compared his vision to works by Orwell, Aldous Huxley, and, to some extent, Borges, Paulo Coelho, and Thomas Mann's *Magic Mountain*.

Elusively written and hard to be pigeonholed in simplistic formulas, Leonard Oprea's writings are truly original and give voice to a unique human experience and sensibility. History and psychology interact in a complex, ineffable, indeed, a mysterious dialogue, and the reader is mesmerized by the author's insightful inroads into the characters' visions, obsessions, fears, and traumas.

In 1999, Leonard Oprea came to the United States. Courageously, I would dare to say heroically, he decided to reinvent himself as an American writer from Central Europe. The books he wrote after his coming to the States (*The Nine Teachings of Theophil Magus on Transylvanian Magic* and *The Book of Theophil Magus or 40 Tales About Man,* as well as *The Meditations of Theophil Magus or Simple Christian Thoughts at the Beginning of the Third Millennium*) were bestsellers with a strong impact on Romanian culture. They came out from Romania's most respected and highly selective Polirom Publishing House.

Leonard Oprea's fictional writings impress me mostly through their narrative power. He is a consummate storyteller, always able to discover deep meanings and implications, constructing unexpected perspectives and detecting, imagining astounding turns of events.

His tell-tale stories from TRILOGY of THEOPHIL MAGUS – *The Truth* (the revised and complete edition of *The Book of Theophil Magus or 40 Tales about Man*) *are situated in a strange no man's land where everyday life becomes truly magical.*

I most enthusiastically define Leonard Oprea's writings as splendid expressions of a uniquely original vision of our fragmented, shattered, but marvelously exciting world. Here we have a truly unique voice, an unparalleled perspective rooted in the bizarre, exotic, but still immensely familiar world of things that are and are not what they promise to be.

Let me just add that Leonard Oprea's American language style combines a discovery of hidden meanings of words with a fabulous sense of secret humor.

Serenely hopeless, these writings are a continuous invitation to soul-searching, self-scrutiny, and admission that the world's deepest meaning lays in the ubiquitous presence of a hidden transcendence (what Arthur Koestler called the "invisible writing" or the "language of destiny").

Leonard Oprea's book will be for the American reader a fresh, uninhibited, genuinely different voice, and I most cordially urge you to listen to it.

***

(*Vladimir Tismaneanu* – philosopher, author, essayist and editor, professor of the University of Maryland / Washington DC, 2008)

THE STORY OF THEOPHIL MAGUS

I come to God and ask Him:

'Lord, please make me a writer!'

God mimics:

'. . . make me a writer . . .' then curtly and clearly: 'Why? Elaborate!'

I do not waver.

You don't play games with God.

I draw a really big circle. Inside it I draw a rose with eight perfectly rounded petals that touch each other.

And in each of these petals I write five tales with swiftness and composure.

They are tales about all sorts of people and the questions that beset them.

But also tales about saints and children, about old people and their loneliness, about Edgar Allan Poe and Mahatma Gandhi, about tigers, bears, foxes, crows, and eagles.

About Jesus Christ and the world of Lazarus, about journalists and witches, about Native Americans and Buddha.

About a math teacher and a national hero, about how to make yourself a library, about how a hermit-writer and a monk-critic drive away the winter, about tearing the cat in two.

About Moses and Death, about the perfectly normal Quidam and Jacob's ladder.

About a wise dwarf and a peasant in the Twilight Zone, about far-from-doubting Thomas the Apostle, about Rabbis and their Itzaks, about . . . all things.

A genuine yet carefully patterned hodge-podge about God and the world.

In each of the eight rose petals I draw a key for every cycle of five tales. It looks like the eight secret ways to Heaven's Gate.

Then I quickly stand on the edge of the really big circle of my 40 tales and I tell God:

'There it is, Lord.'

God looks at it carefully. He seems to be smiling. He starts to pace slowly and randomly through the world of my rose.

Then He rests by my side on the edge of the circle. He grumbles something. Eventually, He utters sternly:

'This is not a joke!'

I suddenly feel sick and mumble:

'But, Lord, how else can I tell the Tale?'

'O.K. I'll make you a writer!' God cuts me short.

I feel even sicker, but I still dare ask:

'Then who's going to read me, Lord?'

God is suddenly cheered:

'Me! But only if you help yourself – get it?'

I do, but I pretend not to.

God frowns:

'I am Who I am ! You have to help yourself !'

***

There it was. I gathered my tales in a book.

Then I found myself a publisher.

And I'm calling the readers.

I must please God.

(Theophil Magus)

CHAPTER 1

"This is the disciple who is bearing witness to these things,
and who has written these things;
and we know that his testimony is true."
(John 21/ 24)

***

Lord, bless my tales!
Thank you, my God!

A TALE OF HOW TO DRIVE THE WINTER AWAY

It all came to pass once upon a wondrous time, or they would not be telling this tale, and tell it they shall in times to come.

Once in this strange wide world, so wide and strange that the Earth can hardly hold it and the Lord Himself can hardly fathom it, there lived two brothers who were uncannily unlike each other. There was no resemblance between them in either frame or countenance, for they were neither of the same mother, nor of the same father. They lived not in the same city and ate not the same dish. They were of different ages, and had different wives and children. Yet in their heart, soul, and mind they knew themselves to be good brothers, so the Lord Himself counted them as brothers. One of them made up countless tales, the other endlessly conceived tales about tales. People would gossip about the former and laughingly call him the Hermit. The latter, people would talk about and grin and call him the Monk. The Hermit and the Monk rarely saw one another.

In plain words, they met once a year and half spoke once a year. Still, the Hermit knew by heart the Monk's tales about tales, as the Monk knew the Hermit's tales. And they did yet one other thing for their kin that was peculiar, to wit, they helped one other to the best of their abilities, but always in wayward and secret ways, staying clear of the world's faithless desire to try and estrange a man from any good and useful deed.

But the two brothers were hiding deep in the recess of their heart a yearning to meet and at least once in their life to talk to their heart's full, tell one another about their worries.

They were never to live to see that happen – just and unfathomed be forever the ways of our Lord.

But the Hermit and the Monk did finally meet as they had always wished – in the next world, when they died.

There they were, every bit the same, rather short, bellies nicely rounded, bearded, tanned, eyes like long almonds, greedy lips and restless looks, just as they had been when they were alive, and sitting at a table full of that world's bounteousness, sipping of God's refreshing, incense-bearing wine, carried away with their long-spun chat. Even they could not say for how long. But it felt so good, and many a time had they prayed in speech or in though for this to be their eternity.

For, you see, the Hermit and the Monk ended up still tale spinning, even after their death. Only now it was from one to the other. And their story was endless and livelier as it failed to reach an end. At times, the Lord Himself would eavesdrop on their tale.

But one fair day, the Hermit said:

'I had a dream last night.

I was back on Earth. Everything was as it had always been before I died, yet recognize people or places I could not. My wife knew me, my children knew me, you knew me, people knew me.

I conducted myself as before, kept on making up tales and was called the Hermit, as before.

before, kept on making up tales and was called the Hermit, as before. But I could not recognize anything. It was much like a winter of no beginning and no end.

Each snow keeps changing the same winter endlessly. And I kept wondering whether mine are the tales of a hermit or whether I am the hermit of tales.'

The Monk fell a-thinking for a long, long while, then replied with a slight lisp, as he was known to do, mostly to his brother:

'In my other life I once went on a journey, far away from my city. I went to Asia. And you know very well I was never too fond of the yellowish little people, with their slanted eyes and hiding inside themselves like a tortoise in its shell. Perhaps I did not like them because they were too much like myself. You know, the tortoise . . . Let me plainly confess I had always wanted to live in the memory of my city as a Chinese Wall. No matter. During my stay with them, I learned the tale of one Takuan. Hear this:

"A drop of time passed. Here lies the most precious diamond. The day that passed. When will I know how to sip again the same drop? That instant shall be the priceless diamond."'

The Hermit remained as silent as a flake of a snow – another in the same winter.

The Monk lisped quietly:

'Brother, let us drive away the winter.'

And the Lord sent them back on Earth and unhermited the one and unmonked the other. He replaced their soul and mind, and filled them with heart and spirit.

And He left them their tales.

To carry them around into the world.

To drive away the winter.

A TALE OF CHRISTMAS

The news of their return had spread across the city. From the King and his knights to the last servant, men and women were all animated by the announcement. The priests alone frowned and called for God's Word to validate their distrust. But nobody paid any attention to them. The same question and the same hope, the same fear and relief, the same laughter and the same tears tormented the souls of swineherd and king alike.

The years had gone by with endless wars, with famine and plagues, with frosts and dry seasons, years that looked like the end of the world – such read the chronicles.

The hermits sighed and the whole city prayed for the redemption that the two chosen men could bring.

For the Magus and the Errant Knight had been sent, as foretold by the wise men of yore, to seek and fetch the Effigy and the Epitaph, which alone could provide the key to any living soul's redemption. For in the face of Death, as everyone knew, we all stand equal.

In vain had the priests tried to prophecy, '. . . it is as it should be, your sins made God turn His face from you . . .', for they too had dishonored the Scriptures. The people, from swineherd to king, knew only too well that the priests had lied, cursed, ended the lives of their own brethren. They knew only too well that the Lord has His own ways and that the chosen ones are but few. Nevertheless they had all been praying, though it seemed it was too late. So that, finally, driven mad by the terror, they had decided. They sent the Magus and the Errant Knight to seek out their redemption – the Effigy and the Epitaph.

It was snowing tiny flakes that swirled with the frail breath of the wind and it was sunny and the next day was Christmas. A good omen, they said and laughed at their luck. They had all gathered outside the city gates: the king and knights were all dressed in marten and ermine fur, purple velvet, diamonds and sapphires, the people had washed their hands, face and necks, had combed their hair that still swarmed with lice, and were wearing their awkward best for the occasion, and there was fretting and restlessness outside the city gates. By order of his majesty the king, the innkeepers offered wine and sausages, the jesters tumbled in the snow, and all, all yearned for redemption.

Pigs and chickens sneaked through the legs of the crowd. Legs that kicked. The sudden squeals and various cries merged with the peals of laughter in a strange humming mirth that floated all around with the snowflakes in the sunlight. Suddenly there was silence, except for the scarce cockcrow, dog snarl, or the soft neighing. Then the field of undisturbed white and the dark deep forest nearby froze.

The two reached the magnificent gray stone arch of the gates. They dismounted in front of the king. A short simple bow. The Magus: tall and thin, worn tunic and ragged cloak. The magic stick alone looked the same. The Errant Knight: strong, rough looks and aging face, yet quiet and proud in his scratched armor. The sword alone seemed to throb in his closed fist. The king returned their greeting and ordered them to speak. They took turns to tell their quiet tale, each showing in strikingly simple words, so masterly chosen, how they had traveled the whole wide world and how they had managed, together, to return safely from their quest, for the Effigy and the Epitaph had unimaginably powerful protectors and keepers.

Clear and resounding, their words stirred the souls, like bowstrings ready to snap.

Finally, the king demanded the unequivocal result. And everything went deaf, for such was the depth of the silence.

The glowing eyes of the Magus and the clear eyes of the Errant Knight met. No one saw their faint smile like a snowflake melting on feverish lips.

'Speak!' the royal summons was heard once again, and the crowd took an eager step towards the two men.

'Wait!' came their tired advice.

Instantly, the Magus raised his magic stick and the Errant Knight drew a circle with his sword.

What were they going to do – kill each other now, in the hour of their redemption?!

Now that the found Effigy and Epitaph had bestowed angelic powers on them? They all gasped, from king to swineherd. But the Magus turned on his heels unexpectedly and pointed his stick at his side of the crowd. And the sword whisked to the side of the Errant Knight.

'Wait!' the two men's voices lashed the air.

A few women yielded subdued cries, a few knights pulled at the reigns and their steeds rose on their hind legs and neighed.

'Wait!' and the two took a quick charging step, then another.

The crowd shrunk back, hundreds of throbbing hearts, eyes rolling like those of terrified cattle, all the same, all at once.

The Magus straightened up and brought down his magic stick. The Errant Knight subdued his sword and quietly turned his back on them.

'We have spoken', their rocky whisper reached the crowd.

The two men mounted.

The sound of the flying hoofs. For a while, there was nothing but the flying hoofs, dying away.

Eventually, came a late curse. Then another, – then the others. And the whizzing of the flying stones. And the soldiers spurring their horses. The Knights balancing their lances. The priests rushing in front of the crowd, raising the Cross. And may God and may the sins . . .

The Magus and the Errant Knight melted in the distance like two ghosts, estranged by the fury of blind terror. Yet protected by the play of the snowflakes, by the undisturbed silence of the field and the forest, by the Effigy and the Epitaph. By the Christmas Eve. Amen.

THE TALE OF ONE ABUL-HASSAN

Midday in Baghdad, the city of one of mighty Harun al-Rashid's descendants.

In the shadow of the white wall, eyes closed, the ancient dervish is listening to Abul-Hassan. When he is done talking, the old man half opens his eyes and stares at him. Finally, he drawls out:

'May Allah protect you! Somewhere in the endless desert there is the Oasis-of-the-Wisest-of-the-Wise. First, do stop and *think it over for a lifetime as it appears to you just before dying*. Only then may you go search the oasis, and find it you will.'

Saying this, the dervish drops his dry eyelids. He starts muttering a religious chant. Faintly he nods. Abul-Hassan understands he is not going to learn more here. He bows to the old man. He carefully picks his words to thank him. He leaves behind an offering of dates, figs, and honey cakes heaped in the lap of the dervish. He bows again. He leaves.

For days on end Abul-Hassan wanders through the streets and market places of Baghdad questioning other dervishes, and scholars, merchants, and warriors whether they have ever heard about the Oasis-of-the-Wisest-of-the-Wise. But he receives no explanation. Some, though, with a compassionate look in their eyes, offer useful advice about traveling across the endless desert. He is told how to prepare to face thirst, how to resist the scorching days and freezing nights, how to confront the storms and the thieves of the sands, but mostly he is told how to guide himself by the stars and what roads to take. Abul-Hassan thanks them all heartily and repays the less fortunate with a golden dinar.

In less than two weeks, Abul-Hassan is ready to set out on his journey.

On the eve of his departure, as he paces the cool garden of his house, Abul-Hassan feels his soul pierced by misgivings he has never experienced before. He thinks that soon, in a couple of months, he may find solace. He remembers the long years of bitterness, when he tried to shelter, protect, and organize his scores of books and manuscripts, so none would ever perish.

The moon is shining above the garden when Abul-Hassan starts wringing his hands. Suddenly he feels chilly. He goes to bed.

He is unable to sleep, instead he decides he is not going to leave before he has *thought it over for a lifetime as it appears to you just before dying*. Although he humbly acknowledges that he has no idea what that meant.

At dawn, he takes his prayer carpet and withdraws to the coolest chamber in the house. He has ordered not to be disturbed by anyone; the caliph is to be told he is already on his way. The only human allowed to enter his chambers once a day to bring water is his youngest son, a boy of three, who has not yet been maculated by sins.

For days on end Abul-Hassan strives to gather the meaning of the old dervish's words.

One morning he comes out of his room and having leisurely eaten a couple of dates, he drinks some wine mixed with goat milk, orders his servants to take the saddles off the camels and unpack his things. Then he steps into the room where his books are carefully stored. He stops in front of the door for a few minutes. Finally, he goes in. He looks around the room for countless moments. And slowly, slowly he comes to understand there is no one there but himself.

He smiles.

Then he bows.

A TALE OF REVELATION

All his life, Itzak Abramovich had been a decent, honorable man. He had looked after his family and his clock repair shop, so that only a few odd people could ever find anything to reproach and gossip when it came down to him. Moreover, Itzak Abramovich stuck to his daily prayer, always ate kosher, observed the Sabbath, read the Holy Books, went to the synagogue – in short, he was one who feared God.

All was fine and to a good purpose, until one morning when Itzak Abramovich burst into the rabbi's office. The rabbi's secretary was desperately hanging from his arm, but nothing in the world could have stopped Itzak Abramovich.

The rabbi saw the wild countenance and the gleaming eyes of the decent and honorable clock-maker, so with a brief gesture he dismissed his secretary who left the room, quietly closing the door behind him.

'Why, Itzak Abramovich, what a pleasure. Come, don't just stand there, I'm not going to bite. It's been quite a while now, hasn't it? Please, sit. There . . . Now, whatever is the matter, Itzak? Would you like a glass of water? You may even smoke, if it is any comfort . . .'

'Rabbi! O, Rabbi, I had a dream!'

The rabbi sighed with relief. 'Praise the Lord, there is no tragedy here', he told himself and, running his fingers through his thin, ash-gray beard, he sank in his armchair.

'Do tell, my dear Itzak, do tell. What dream?'

'Rabbi, last night I had a wonderful dream . . . Wonderful and frightening, Rabbi.

I cannot tell . . . I lived a quiet life for fifty years and, look now, just last night . . . Forgive me, Rabbi, but if I hadn't come to see you, I would have gone crazy . . .'

'All right, all right, but tell me all about it, my dear Itzak', the rabbi smiled.

'Rabbi, last night I dreamt Jacob's Ladder.'

'And – what was it like?'

'Well – everything the book says . . . "And he dreamed, and behold a ladder set up on the earth, and the top of it reached to heaven: and behold the angels of God ascending and descending on it."

The rabbi could read terror in the eyes of Itzak Abramovich and he cut him short authoritatively:

'And what were you doing there, Itzak?'

'Frankly, Rabbi, at first I just stood there staring – it was so beautiful . . . And all the angels ascending and descending . . . Then, I don't know what came over me, I had this sudden urge and braced myself and went sneaking through the angels, hiding behind them, then I started ascending. I was careful to stick to the middle of the ladder – it had no railings and I have this fear of heights . . .'

Itzak Abramovich stopped, swallowed a few times, looked at the rabbi, saw him calm and smiling, so he went on with his dream:

'So there I was – climbing, excited, not too frightened though, rather happy, I told myself I may get to see God . . . I ascended for a long time. But suddenly, I don't know what came over me and I looked around: the angels kept ascending and descending – there's so many of them, Rabbi . . . but there was nothing besides them and the ladder. Nothing at all. Only a white light, like an endless curtain of pure water through which you can see a long way in the distance – you can see just that . . . Rabbi . . . and I really wanted to see God so much, but I was seized with such fear . . . God, such a terrible fear! Rabbi, I thought I was going to die, I was so scared!'

'All right, Itzak. Come, now, calm down. Go on, tell me', the rabbi sighed.

'I don't know, Rabbi . . . But I couldn't stand the terror and I started to run madly. All I could see was that the angels somehow seemed to make room for me . . . and it seemed, really, Rabbi, that God Himself called out to me not to be afraid . . . But I was so terrified that I ran even harder. And the closer I got to the ground the more I prayed that God help me reach you sooner, Rabbi, that you may help me . . . And when I woke up I was so horrified that I even said my prayers in a hurry that I may rush here to you . . .'

The hands of Itzak Abramovich had started to fly around, his lips were quivering, and the rabbi saw that it was fit he should tell him:

'Do calm yourself, my dear Itzak Abramovich. Enough,' he shouted, 'you are alive, you are awake, and you are not going to die too soon, seeing that you are a decent, honorable man, and I will pray for you. Enough!'

Itzak Abramovich froze like a first grader who got caught with a poorly written homework and, on top of it, furtively eating the sandwich he had forgotten about while playing during the break.

'Very well, Itzak. Look, you are here, safe and sound. Yet I cannot but feel there is something else on your mind. Come, tell', the rabbi invited him.

'Please, Rabbi, tell me, for I wronged no one in fifty years, is this a sign . . .'

The rabbi looked at Itzak Abramovich very intensely, then he placed his hand over the man's hand, on the side of the desk and spoke in a slow, fatherly voice:

'My dear Itzak, confess to me, how did that ladder seem to you?'

'Endless, Rabbi. And I was so lonely . . .'

'You see, Itzak, had you felt differently, your dream would have been a revelation. But as things stand, it was just a dream.'

'O, Rabbi, what a relief', Itzak smiled the tears making his voice coarse.

'Just a dream', the rabbi smiled candidly.

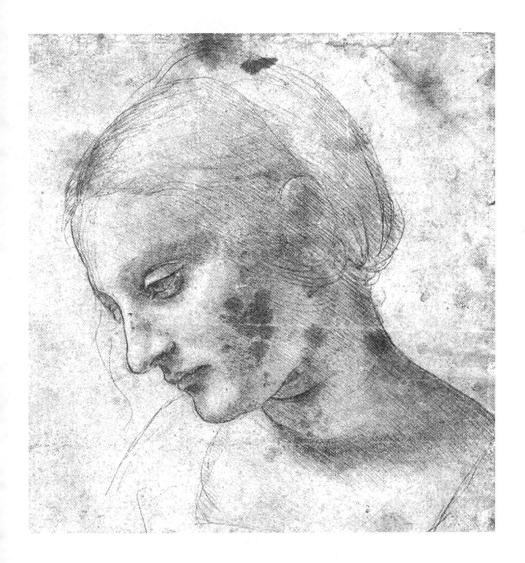

A TALE OF THE HOLY EASTER

Mary had kept those words in her heart where she thought about them. There could have been no other way as the Archangel Gabriel and Elisabeth and old Simon had recognized her and had blessed her forever. But there was something else old Simon had said . . . And Mary shuddered once more as she pronounced them to herself: . . . *even if your soul be run through by a sword, that the thoughts of many hearts may be uncovered* . . . And Mary had seen and known everything. She had heeded, learned and gathered the burden of the Light for ten, twenty, indeed, maybe thirty years during the late nights, by the flickering candle with her child, the modest carpenter, beside her and the teacher, Rabboni . . .

***

And it was spring. And it was the feast of Easter. And it was little before the sixth hour on the Place of the Skull. The sun had gone pale, clouds were gathering and a soft, humid mist stifled the breath. On her knees, Mary appeared to the world like a carved agony. But she kept all those words – kept them alive in her heart. The One, whose eyes were burnt with the terror and awe of human death. Although she knew. Drained, Mary the Mother stood there petrified in front of her Son, her carpenter, the child killed by the scholars, by whose people? God's? she asked herself as if she, Mary, was the one crucified. And she prayed with all her heart, with all her soul, with all her mind, with all the strength of her being: No, my Lord . . . My Lord wherefore do you forsake me? No, my Lord, forsake me not!

***

And it was spring. And it was the feast of Easter. And it was little after the ninth hour on the Place of the Skull. Darkness had fallen upon the land. And yet each man could see. And in the Temple the curtain had been torn from top to bottom. And each man could hear.

Mary alone looked like a second cross, raised in front of Christ. Crucified by Christ's words, the One on the Cross of the World: *see that your hearts become not heavy with the food and the drink and the worries of this life, or that day shall come unexpectedly upon you.* His words alone started the healing of the clay creature, Mary.

Mary alone felt then, as if the Heavens, the air, the earth, and the waters had been kneaded with blood and Light, that she is overcome by her child's cry, the One who had been humiliated and killed: *E'lo-i, E'lo-i, la'ma sabach-tha'ni?*

But in the Place of the Skull, the Jews, the Romans and the men of other nations only felt a deep, inscrutable fear, like hundreds of blind, dumb, and deaf ants on a rocking anthill.

***

John's arm enveloped Mary's shoulders when the spear ran through the chest of Jesus.

At that very moment, when blood and water gushed out of the wound, marking, forgiving, and redeeming the place and the people, Mary was awaken by His drops that touched her. She looked up and she saw the smile in the light of the eyes of the Crucified. Jesus Christ was smiling to Mary.

And the Virgin Mary heard the call like a chiding commandment: *Thou shalt not fear . . . ,* as she had done before the Birth.

And John the apprentice at once said to her:

'Come, Mother. He shall not orphan us; He shall return. Let us wait for Him properly.

CHAPTER 2

Oh, yes – too many times you feel like an empty shell in the tide.

It seems there is no hope . . .

And no one can help you . . .

Yet, Jesus the Christ died on the cross for your sins and

resurrected for your re-birth.

Therefore, do not give up.

Just look for Jesus into your heart.

You will see . . . the truth.

And the truth will make you free, said Jesus.

(Theophil Magus)

THE TALE OF A TALE TELLER

Although he lived at the end of the twentieth century of our era and was past his first youth, he never felt tales were something unnatural. He rather thought of them as simple, clear, beneficial, and always needed. He had often considered that maybe it was time for the tales of his times to be written. He felt it was only natural that the tale be eternally reborn. And he even bravely voiced this view in front of all his friends. Naturally, they all thought he was out of his wits. For people were surrounded and besieged by micro- and macro-computers, by outer space flights, by nuclear missiles and cruise missiles, by hunger, by sex, by pollution, by unhappy marriages, by cancer and the flu and AIDS, by psychoanalysis, by dictatorships and democracies, by economic and political treaties, by books that drove you crazy with their analysis of artistic form, and their dissection of social structures. At best, they were indifferent to his ways of feeling and thinking. But he never felt tales were anything unnatural.

It was the end of the winter of I forget which year of his life, which, as with all great lovers of tales, seemed to stretch inordinately behind and ahead. One morning with ice flowers on windows, just as he had put down a book of tales and was staring stupefied at the beautiful frost orchids, it occurred to him that he must find a princess and nestle her in his feeble arms (they weren't really that feeble, but this is what is commonly believed of tale tellers) and caress her 'with silk fingers and with whispering butterfly wings'; and then 'summon with a sigh a dream of a lagoon with corals and colorful fish, while happily falling asleep'.

This is what occurred to him and with eyes dimmed by fantasies he went on staring at the orchids, which meanwhile had turned into ice roses and chrysanthemums. The book had fallen from his knees on to the carpet. Suddenly he wondered whether he was entitled to sleep in the company of a princess, for he was after all no more than a common man. And then a bluish mist floated into his room. And at the same time the phone started ringing. And it buzzed and buzzed.

He was incapable of moving from his couch. The bluish mist had already enveloped him (great tale tellers are usually pictured as myopic, lame, full of pimples, frustrated by their physical defects), clothed him in a mantle of light, gave him an aura of pure thoughts, and turned him as beautiful as the saints of yore. Then the princess materialized from that mist and that blue. Her countenance was such that the taleteller gasped for breath. The princess smiled mysteriously, embraced him, and started to caress him. He felt he was soon going to cry with joy.

The phone was ringing in frenzy.

The princess reached for the receiver and placed it to his ear. He heard a voice spelling:

'Good day. It's me, the Princess. My name is immaterial for I am the Princess. Be advised that I forbid myself to sleep with you: First, I have such a vast life experience that I cannot believe in this innocent sleep as you imagine it.

Second, my life turned me into an incredibly moral and fair person.

Third, as a mature princess with a good deal of self-respect, I have my own family, a husband and children. The children have grandparents, and lots of other relatives and friends. My friends have their own families. And I work for a living. So there are also my work associates. So start from this and think about the other two points I made and lose the notion of silk fingers and such nonsense. What you really want is sex. Don't forget I am a princess and I will not risk my life foolishly. Here's my advice. Take it. *A soul you shut off yourself and the stagnant peace will give you moral strength and happiness.* Be sensible. It is true, mature princesses, worthy of respect, do have to take a chance, occasionally. But not like that. Maybe there are a few world-orphan princesses left somewhere out there. Seek them out if you really must have a princess. But I recommend that you stop your vagrancy in the realm of tales. And, another thing, except for yourself and a few other loonies, no one thinks of us as princesses anymore. Not even ourselves. And that is because we became social beings. Good bye.

The princess had long hung up. The great tale lover stared dumbfound at the woman in his arms. Just as enchanting and with the same mysterious smile, she touched his forehead with her fingers. 'Princess', he muttered as she disappeared in the blue whence she had materialized.

Moments elapsed like ages. The silence and the peace of death thoughts plugged the ears of the tale lover. Finally, he sighed and the room vibrated with the faint moaning of a flute.

The man wiped off a tear that was sliding down to his quivering lips and spoke out loudly: 'May the tale protect her!' The bluish mist was still with him. It embraced him, rocked him, and brought sleep to his eyelids. It watched him for a while, then gathered into a drop of clear sky and entered his soul. There it unfolded once more as the room with ice flowers on the windows.

And out of the blue rose the Princess.

The phone was no longer on the small table by the couch.

**

The tale lover smiled in his sleep as the Princess nestled in his arms and happily fell asleep.

It all came to pass one winter day at the end of the twentieth century of our era.

THE TALE OF THE DAUGHTER OF TIME

Time summoned Death, stroked her brow, and looking into her eyes said:

'My child, you are immortal and you are everywhere. And this is the very reason for which you love oblivion more than anyone else. Yet, you, even you, must remember you are alive.'

'Father . . . please . . .' Death whispered.

'Go!' Time commanded.

***

On her way back from school, near the trunk of the blooming lilac, in the raw grass, the girl found a dead sparrow chick. She bent down and took the little bird in the scoop of her palms. She stroked her wings and her fluffy chest. Her eyes got misty. Careful not to unsettle the chick, she took it to the garden of her parents' house. There, in the earth, she made a nest for it. She placed the chick inside, covered it with dust mixed with grass and chamomile flowers and prayed for a miracle to bring it back to life. She arranged the roof of dust, grass, and flowers such that the little sparrow might push it aside and fly away. When she was done, she smiled contented and went about her childish business.

***

At dawn the young sparrow flew away. It came to the blooming lilac. It landed in the grass around the tree trunk and died.

***

On her way back from school, the little girl found the dead sparrow. She bent down and took it in the scoop of her palms. Then with misty eyes she went on and did the same as the day before.

***

At dawn the young sparrow came back to life, then died as it had done the previous days. But the little girl no longer showed up. She had died.

***

Time summoned Death, stroked her brow, and looking into her eyes asked:

'Have you performed your duty, my child?'

'Yes, father,' Death whispered. 'I remembered I am immortal, I am everywhere, and – I am alive. But, again, each time I have to do it, I wish I could die.'

THE TALE OF THE HERO

And the hero was surrounded by enemies. He fought like a god, like an angel. But they were as many as the grass leaves. And he could not die a heroic death, as he would have wanted, as it would have fit his dignity and his nature.

He was taken prisoner.

The world public opinion zoomed in on it. What was to be done with the Hero? Execution would have turned him into a martyr; a life sentence of hard labor would have meant thousands of convicts admiring him, protecting him. That would have brought in reporters to augment the story on TV and radio, peace and environmental organizations, and who knows what other kinds of trouble. It was decided that the Hero be given a forced domicile in a castle on top of the mountains.

***

Years went by. Peace set in. And then they remembered the Hero.

The case was re-discussed.

The Hero had to be released.

One fairly sunny morning, the Hero had to leave the old castle that had meant a decent life for him. He felt somewhat uneasy about the release. He had grown accustomed with life at the castle.

True enough, there had been other moments when he did remember he was a prisoner after all.

There had been moments during his siesta, or while relaxing with a mistress, or at the end of a hunt offered by the governor of the castle, or while admiring from the top of the buttresses the snow-clad peaks in the sunset, when he wondered whether 'freedom' was not really a rather obscure word.

There had also been moments when he meditated on the duties of a hero.

Well, he had grown accustomed with life at the castle.

And he felt somewhat uneasy about the release.

***

He embraced the flooded-eyed governor and pressed him against his broad, sinewy chest.

They sank in the scarlet leather armchairs.

They lit their Cubans. They smoked for a while in silence.

Every now and then they sipped their perfumed cognac from the big-bellied glasses.

Eventually, the governor informed the Hero with emotion in his voice that he had been awarded an honorary citizen diploma.

The Hero extended his warm gratitude and decided he was leaving the next day. The governor invited him for a good-bye dinner and the Hero offered him one of his medals.

***

A year had passed since the release. Meanwhile, the Hero had traveled throughout the country.

And the country whose hero he had once been, declared war against the country he was now in.

And invaded it.

The Hero found himself tormented by dark thoughts. If he stayed he would have to confront the invader, which was his call, but then his former country would hold him for a lowly traitor. If he went back to his country after so many years and in wartime he would no doubt be taken for a dangerous spy and not be allowed to fight for his country.

What was he to do?!

Neutrality was out of the question for, after all, he was a hero.

He then decided: a hero can only be a hero if he fights – on the battlefield – for a just cause. And it has always been the case that invaders are waging unjust wars. Now this country is being invaded.

Just as the other homeland had been years ago.

***

In this battle the Hero was surrounded by enemies. So many that, although he fought like a god, like an angel, he could not die a heroic death, as he would have wanted, as it would have fit his dignity and his nature.

He was taken prisoner.

As he was an admired public figure worldwide, they could not easily sentence him to death as a traitor, nor treat him as a regular prisoner.

A fortress on top of the mountains became his forced domicile.

***

Years went by. Peace set in. Inside the fortress, the Hero was now leading an entirely civilized life. He had grown accustomed to it. But he had been thinking increasingly often about the castle where he had lived a similar life. And he had been meditating about the meaning of freedom and the duties of a hero.

***

One day he escaped.

***

He wandered through the woods for a fortnight.

***

One summer afternoon he was following a deer when he reached a bright glade. In front of him there were two groups of soldiers each commanded by an officer. Before he knew it, they fell upon each other. So there was a new war. He drew his sword and summoned them to cease the struggle. Nobody listened. He ran from one side to the other shouting at them. Then he was attacked. He defended himself. But they attacked him again. This went on until nothing could be heard except for the voices of the wood.

Long moments passed as the Hero stared wildly at the corpses.

Suddenly, he yelled that someone take him prisoner. Somewhere a crow cried, a scold shrieked, a secret creature puffed.

The Hero haunted the woods sniffing for the war. Wanting to be made a prisoner. Hungry, tattered, pale, and with dark circles around his eyes, he looked like a ghost.

Flea-ridden and delirious with fever, he came upon a hamlet. The mountain people gave him shelter and looked after him until he recovered. He now looked as impressive as in his days of glory, his eyes shining as those of a god or an angel.

One day his hosts told him the Hero had been taken prisoner and is now living in a castle on top of the mountains. He was petrified.

He fretted all day and all night, until he felt inside an endless desert.

In the morning he greeted the people in the house. They stared speechless at the shaking old man in front of them. He never got to eat his bread and drink his milk.

He died slowly dropping his head onto the course plank of the table.

The priest told the mountain people that a man growing old over night and dying suddenly could only be the work of the devil.

So they buried him without a cross outside the hamlet, at the edge of the woods, under a yellow rock.

Years went by . . .

***

The yellow rock at the edge of the woods was called the Unholy Rock. Those who know its story stay wide clear of it and cross themselves when they are around that place.

Only the children who drive their sheep by that place find rest there and sometimes they even sleep peacefully in the shadow of that rock.

THE TALE OF A PILGRIM

He had left as a young boy for he could not contain his desire to see and learn things.

Before he left, he had prepared himself for the journey by studying some of the languages of this world and especially by meditating days on end on the counsels he drew from the reports of other pilgrims: "wherever you are strive to live, to feel, and to think as if you were born there".

He had crossed many lands and seas. Some parts of the world he had stayed for as much as two or three years. When about to tread the land of another nation, he always tried to learn in advance its customs, its nature, its teachings, its sorrows, its pleasures, and its dreams. He had earned his food, clothes, and travel money by working in the villages, cities, and harbors where he stopped. And in time he came to know many people, men and women alike, and to learn many trades. Years of pilgrimage added up and increased his wisdom.

He was now by the side of the road, next to a cross. He had drunk the clear cold water from the well. Then he cooled himself washing his hands, face, and feet. He had eaten of the food he carried in his bag. And had once more drunk of the clean, fresh water.

Sitting on the thick green grass around the cross he puffed at his old pipe. With a touch of blue and fragrance, the smoke rose in lazy twists.

The pilgrim was staring at the top of the hill. In the valley beyond lied the town of his birth.

He had sat there for more than two hours, letting his mind drift with the various thoughts, now foaming like the rapids, now quiet as the big rivers. A few travelers passed by, yet none dared disturb the man with the silver hair and beard, the man whose face was the icon of Time.

Sometimes, the eyes of the pilgrim lit suddenly and a small tear rolled like a glass marble down the sunburned, wind-carved cheek.

Sometimes his hands shook with their bulging knuckles and twining veins.

A couple of times his smothered sighs broke out in the singing silence.

Soon the sun would set.

The man's soul was overcome by doubt. The road cut across the hill as if the back of a dark leviathan had been severed in two.

The eyes of the pilgrim had long been arrested by the vacant stare. And the sun, so round and full, sucked under or bursting from the cut in the hill . . . or God knows what . . .

The two trees on each side of the sun, one almost entirely dry, the other with thousands of leaves, none of them set on fire by the blood red horizon . . .

One more sunset, he thought.

He rose, picked up his bag, his stick, and walked away.

Behind him, nothing was left of the sun but the dying ashes.

And a deserted town.

THE TALE OF THE FIVE PRINCIPLES

The Lord our Father made man out of the dust of the earth, blew the breath of life into his nostrils and man became a living soul.

And God looked at man and saw that he lacked something without which His work was imperfect.

Then God said:

Nothing comes by accident.

And He made for man his little finger. Man moved it.

Then God said:

Let good and bad find you only when you have denied Me.

And He made for man his ring finger. Man moved it. And God saw that it moved.

Then God said:

Nothing is purposeless.

And He made for man his middle finger. Man moved it.

Then God said:

May you not fight against your fate except through Me, your Lord God.

And He made for man his index finger. Man moved it. And God looked at it carefully.

Then God said:

May you be powerless without your faith in God.

And God made for man his thumb. Man moved it. Then he saw that he had hands with which he can do a lot of things. Man was beside himself with joy, yet he did ask:

'Lord, how may I thank you?'

God was silent.

Man grew sad and prayed:

'Lord, you gave me a living soul and hands with five fingers. You gave me the five principles. Now test me.'

Then God said:

'Let it be so.'

And God made man his woman.

Then He loosed the snake into the world.

CHAPTER 3

To be yourself – what does that mean?!
How can you be yourself, since you do not know who you really are?
How to discover who you really are?
Yes – searching for the truth.
What is the truth?
God said to Moses: I am Who I am.
Yes . . . Therefore,
I think you need a human answer.
Find Jesus the Christ.

(Theophil Magus)

A TALE OF FRIENDSHIP

The two friends came into the yard. One told the other:

'I have called you to show you something remarkable! Look!' he said and called his dog, a beautiful Scottish shepherd.

The dog came quickly, happily wagging his tail. His master patted him on the head and told his friend:

'Look at his eyes, they are covered with a white film. See? He has gone blind. He is old and his sight is gone.'

Then he waved his hand in front of the dog's eyes, and the dog didn't as much as blink.

'See? He is blind as a bat. I heard I can have him operated, but to make him really see, I have to get him glasses or contact lenses. But he is just a dog, and a dog can't wear these things. So he is doomed to remain blind. But watch this!" He started playing with the dog. The dog moved naturally, without hesitation. Then his master ordered him to jump, to fetch, to lie down, to attack, and many other things. The dog performed each trick with gusto. His master's sharp voice had a miraculous effect on the dog.

Finishing his demonstration, the owner asked his friend laughing happily:

'Well, what do you think? Do you realize how strong his smell and hearing are? And how much he loves me?'

'Have you done this everyday since he went blind?' the friend asked.

'No, only occasionally, just so he won't feel abandoned. He is blind anyway.'

'Then I must now leave you forever. I may go blind myself one day.'

And he left. Quickly. Without looking back.

The master was ready to answer. When he opened his mouth, he told the dog:

'Bark!'

A TALE ABOUT MAHATMA GANDHI

Mahatma Gandhi was a man who prayed a lot for other people, no matter who they were and where they came from. This wise man who would walk as if his body, half-mummified by prayer and fasting, was a huge burden for him, this healer of everyone's suffering, be they sick or healthy, had three masters who guided his every step: Jesus Christ, Krishna, and Buddha. And this is what Gandhi confessed to every man who inquired about his faith.

And many were those in the course of Mahatma's life whose curiosity or revolt made them ask how he dared join the word of Jesus Christ with the teachings of Buddha.

And Gandhi would always answer by telling them the same story:

"Weakened and faint from the journeying and the blood-shedding diarrhea caused by pork meat, a dish no wise man or ascetic would touch, a dish that he had been served for dinner in the house of a poor blacksmith, a man from a lower caste whose house no Brahman or gentleman was likely to enter, Buddha was preparing for his death. There, by the side of the road to Kusinagara, in a bush, between two trees, his face westward, his head northward, his right leg under his left leg, lying on the dry soil, Buddha was trying to smile as he was tortured by the pain.

Ananda, who had been his devoted apprentice and servant for 25 years, the most beloved disciple of the Enlightened one, was at his side and watched him, tears in his eyes. Suddenly he could contain himself no longer, and he burst into crying sobs.

'Enough, Ananda,' Buddha reprimanded him. 'It's no more than one death. And you should really rejoice, as it is my last death. I am to arise and you are to take my place in this world. Through me, you will become a savior, the first Bodhisattva. Enough! Please.'

'But Master,' Ananda barely uttered, 'you are the one who gave us the Law and the Way. You gave us the four Noble Truths and the eight steps of the Way. You alone can deliver us from suffering and now you are passing away on the side of the road, in painful agony, like a poor man deserted by everyone, like a pariah! Stay with me, with us, Master! You can do this!'

'Now listen, Ananda. Come closer and listen,' Buddha smiled with sympathy. 'What have I been doing these past 40 years?'

'You traveled all across India and taught the Good Law. You were always there among the people and for the people. Yet I am not certain that they understood.'

'This is not for you to judge, Ananda. First, be a Buddha yourself. But, now, tell me: what do the first four arms or steps of the Way mean to you?'

'Master, the love and heart-felt pity for all creatures are the right attitude, the right speech, the right deeds, the right living.'

'And tell me, Ananda, may you find redemption without them?'

'No.'

'Ananda, show me such a man. Are you the one?'

'No.'

'Ananda, love does not exist through itself.

And the four arms mean that you should love the other as you love yourself. Without suffering, there is no redemption. And your life does not exist without the life of the blacksmith who offered me open-heartedly his dinner. For he believed in me and he offered me his own food, that which compensates his labor and sustains his everyday life. The lotus grows for a long time under the water and its roots are deeply buried into the mud. It takes patience and toiling for the lotus flower to rise above the water. This is the divine flower.'

'*OM! Namo Narayana!*' Ananda humbly bowed.

'Reverence to the Lord our God!' Buddha faintly whispered the same words.

Then with a simple and serene smile he entrusted his soul to the One Lord our God."

THE TALE OF A MIDGET

History tells us that there once lived in Alexandria one Alypus of Alexandria, a midget renowned for his knowledge and wisdom.

The story tells us that one night Alypus had three dreams.

In his first dream he had become the jester and secret counsel of an emperor who ruled the world. The Emperor loved him and treasured his company such that all courtiers and ministers hated Alypus bitterly. But the Emperor guarded the midget's life like his own and, finally, to protect him from the plots of envious people, he locked him up in a castle where Alypus had all he could wish for, yet could never go beyond the tall walls. There, in that castle, he died of old age and, as stipulated in the Emperor's will, a bronze statue was made and set in the yard of the imperial castle, the statue of a midget wearing a wise smile and a fool's cap. In the second dream, Alypus saw himself as a tall and handsome man.

Of course, it was still he, Alypus, and his face, eyes, voice, knowledge, and wisdom were unchanged. Only he was much younger and was wearing a priest's clothes. He was so much respected by the people of that city, which looked a lot like Alexandria, only it was bigger by far, that, in spite of his young age, they anointed him bishop of that city. And nothing would be done in the city without his consent. He came to decide the fate of all things and persons. With the passing years, he became so powerful, that he only ran the Easter and Christmas service and only received the confessions of the most powerful people of the day. He became estranged from ordinary people and believed himself to have been sent on earth by God Himself.

In his late forties and feared by all, he died in the arms of a courtesan from a fit of apoplexy.

In his third dream, Alypus was a giant dwarf. He lived in a legendary land of the dwarfs, somewhere on a wild mountain robed in dark forests, with steep rocks and deep chasms, a mountain whose snow-clad tops were always hidden by the thick mist.

That was the abode of the little men, who dug the entrails of the mountain and who passed on from one generation to another the trade of forging magic swords, spears, and bows, and of guarding magic treasures and ancient secrets. The little men who, for thousands of years, have featured as the mysterious creatures in the tales and legends of our bards and grandparents.

The dwarfs lived and worked happily in that ancient kingdom. And Alypus, the first and only giant dwarf in the history of that kingdom, was the pride of his people. Not only was Alypus as tall as two regular dwarfs and a knee and as powerful as five strong dwarfs, but he had also forged the rock-cutting ring and the mirror that sang as it gave you its crystal-clear reflection. And it was once again Alypus who, together with a band of carefully chosen dwarfs, had faced and slain the dragon that wanted to steel from the dwarfs their most precious gem, the Mountain Diamond. Alypus was a hero whose name and deeds lived on in everyone's memory for centuries. But he died with a heavy heart, for he had no heirs. On account of his size, giant in all respects, no dwarf woman could be his wife, though many loved him dearly.

And during each of his three dreams, Alypus of Alexandria heard the secret voice of one unseen whose whisper encouraged him: 'Choose for yourself.'

In the morning, when he was wide-awake, Alypus dashed to the mirror. And he saw himself as he really was, a nice midget who loved to read a lot and loved to think even more.

He kept thinking of the three dreams for years after that.

One night he invited his best friend for dinner, an old sailor who had seen and heard many things, and had not lived in vain.

When they were done feasting and had licked their fingers with great relish, they sat in front of their glasses, always full of dark and fragrant wine and started to chat. And Alypus told his friend about his three dreams as if he had actually lived them. And he asked his advice.

After a long interval of silence, the old sailor asked him:

'Are you the one who offered me a kingly feast?'

'Yes,' answered Alypus.

'Then why do you need my advice? It means you have already made your choice.'

'Indeed, I thank God He did not burden my soul with more than a nibble of the fruit of temptation. But I still wanted to reassure myself that this was no more than a nibble. A passing one, too. Or maybe not?'

'Choose for yourself,' said the old man.

A TALE FROM THE TWILIGHT ZONE

One afternoon in the month of July, as quivering ghosts danced in the hot air, a hay cart drawn by two horses dragged down the asphalt ribbon that gently swerved among the slow hills. The horses rocked their heads to the muffled rhythm of hooves on the asphalt, and occasionally swung their tails to keep away the swarming flies on their back.

In the cool shade of the fragrant hay behind them, hands hardened by farm work and sunburned, windblown faces, the couple was dozing peacefully in the cart seat. Their bodies rocked imperceptibly as the cart went over an occasional bump in the road. The peasant would pull at his hat, adjust the reins, and gently prompt his horses, while the woman rearranged her headscarf.

Suddenly, something went whizzing by the hay cart.

The woman half opened her eyes. Then she opened them wide.

She nudged her man:

'Did you see that!'

'See what, woman?' he grunted but never opened his eyes.

'See what? Why . . . there was this . . . headless cyclist . . .'

The man snorted his contempt at the female fantasy and decided it was unworthy of an answer.

Eventually, they resumed dozing against the clapping of hooves.

***

Another whiz went past the cart.

The horses snored lightly, but carried on untroubled.

But the woman put her hand to her mouth and gasped with terror:

'Lord almighty, this can't be good! Another one without a head!' and she quickly crossed herself three times.

The peasant retorted with a dispassionate mumble:

'Now, woman, you'd better moisten that scarf on your head.

The heat got to you, that's your sunstroke for you, to be sure', and keeping his eyes closed he resumed his dozing.

The woman hardly had time to give him a piece of her mind when there was another whiz.

This time the woman shrieked with terror:

'O, my God! Look, there goes another one without a head!!!'

The man pulled at the reins.

'Whoa', he stopped his horses.

Without a twitch on his face he stared ahead, then looked at his wife and quietly told his wife:

'You'd better shift the scythe to the other side of the cart.

And let's get a move on, or we'll be still on the road come midnight.'

***

When life and death are separated by a misplaced scythe, be assured that the whole world has sunk into the Twilight Zone.

And do not doubt that this was meant to be and not an iota will be changed from what was written to happen.

Simply shift your scythe to the other side and do not be troubled – like our good peasant in the story.

A TALE ABOUT OUR LORD

The night had enveloped the ghetto.

The sickly twinkle of still burning candlesticks crept through the shutters of the small, crammed, skewed houses.

It was before midnight and the bluish horn of the moon alone smiled coldly to spite the pitch silence.

Itzak stood for a while in the doorway looking at his wife and son sleeping peacefully, then blew out the night-lamp on the shelf, and stepped out into the darkness. He trudged through the foul mud of the by-street grunting and mumbling occasional supplications to God.

Sometimes he stopped and looked around in fear. But there was nobody around. No ruffians, no thieves, no gypsies or other pagans, nor the Golem. He eventually reached the end of the street and thanked God warmly that Rabbi Copel only lived a few steps from his own house.

He cast a searching look around. Nobody. And a deep silence. He quickly stole into the narrow yard. A hen crowed faintly in its sleep.

Itzak knocked timidly, as if suddenly drained of all strength.

After a while he could hear:

'Who's there?' It was the severe, concerned, yet hospitable voice of the rabbi.

'It's me, Itzak', the man barely replied.

The door half-opened. Itzak crept in and froze next to the door-frame. Rabbi Copel lifted his candle to his amber eyes and peered at his guest.

Itzak's forehead was covered with sweat beads and his lower lip was trembling. The rabbi gently took him by the arm and pulled him towards the chair by his table, which was full of books. Itzak sat slowly and let out a deep sigh.

Rabbi Copel clapped his hands. Then he sat in the other chair, at the opposite side of the table.

Without a word, inaudible, Salome appeared next to them and placed two steaming tea glasses on the table. Then she vanished like a puff of smoke.

The seven branches of the candlestick played its secret lights on the dusty volumes.

'Come, tell', the rabbi gently commanded.

'Oy, oy', Itzak wailed, 'my David, oy-oy, my David became a Christian . . . Oy, oy, he listened to that cursed woman . . .'

The rabbi suppressed his sigh:

'Yes, yes', he simply said and stroked his thick beard.

'What shall I do, oy, oy, what shall I do?! . . .' Itzak whined desperately.

Rabbi Copel reached for the Torah, but changed his mind and stood up abruptly and threateningly. Itzak crouched in his chair. But the rabbi's shoulders drooped under the burden of his impotence. He started pacing up and down the low room with small steps.

'Leave, leave, leave', he rapped morosely.

Drained, Itzak trudged towards the door.

As he touched the handle he heard the voice again:

'Come before the Sabbath. I will tell you then', the rabbi let him gulp for air one more time.

For two whole days Rabbi Copel thought and studied. He smoked his pipe under Salome's chiding eyes. He studied and thought and even drank three glasses of black currant liqueur. All under Salome's by now angry glare.

For two days Itzak prayed and prayed and forgot all about his pastry and *braga* business. Sometimes he left God aside and thoroughly cursed his wife and his David. But mostly he agonized over David loosing Rose's dowry, the daughter of Judas the usurer. He even slapped, kicked, and clubbed with the wattle broomstick his prodigal son. But David still looked lovingly upon his father and gladly suffered the sparrow-like hits from his unhappy father. For, come what may, David knew only too well that Itzak would have given his life for him.

For, ultimately our Lord above watches and judges us.

***

Friday around noon, dressed up and stiff as a broomstick, Itzak headed for Rabbi Copel's house.

It was sunny, the mud had dried up on the side street. The grass had sprouted. The song of birds freshly returned from their winter migration interwove with the din of the ghetto preparing for the Sabbath.

Everyone greeted Itzak and no one gave any sign that they had learned about his mishap. But Itzak was quite familiar with the inside of his kin and would look only ahead. He grunted an unintelligible answer to each greeting and the arms of his soul reached out like those of a drowning man to God.

They were facing each other, Itzak and Rabbi Copel, in the light showers of the small room. Occasionally it became brighter with the rays determined to pierce

the loose texture of the black curtains and it looked like a Ghost had petrified the two old men by the seven-branch candlestick.

Rabbi Copel coughed solemnly:

'Itzak, look at me.'

Itzak could not.

'O come now, Itzak,' something gurgled in his voice and made Itzak look straight into his eyes.

And Rabbi Copel smiled half-secretly, half-awkwardly.

'Itzak, my man, God knows I have a son too.'

Itzak started, but went on looking his rabbi straight in the eye.

'There, now you know too. But you'll forget it. As you leave this room you'll forget it for everyone else, but God. Or I'll curse you.'

Itzak quickly nodded with a dutiful, stupid smile.

'Itzak, my Jew, my son also became a Christian . . . O I won't give you the details', he quickly added, as if talking to himself, with a determined yet mitigating voice.

Itzak started rocking in his chair. A faint high wailing sound was coming from the mouth of a fish that suddenly found itself on the shore.

'Shut up!' the rabbi hissed swiftly. 'Shut up and listen', the rabbi gently entreated. 'Shut up, listen, and be obedient.'

The wailing ended, the rocking stopped, Itzak took a deep breath then finished in one gulp the glass full of apricot brandy.

'That's it', the rabbi encouraged him. 'Now look here, I prayed to Him day and night.

I fasted for forty days. Nothing. He never appeared to me. I bit my lip and blessed the punishment He gave me. I looked for deliverance in the sacred rolls, I cured the sick, I helped the poor, I went on pilgrimage to the Great Temple, then I fasted again for forty days . . . And I wished I could die of shame, though no one knew my secret . . . Just Him . . .' He fell silent. He sipped his black currant liqueur from the small silver glass.

Itzak was staring at the rabbi. He had shrunken and looked helpless as he sat in horror with his hands in his lap by the table full of dusty volumes.

The Rabbi drew near him, put his hands on his shoulders and shook him up strongly:

'Come, Itzak, come, for the Lord watches from up there . . . He did appear to me the day after I blessed my son. I saw and heard Him. Though I can't really tell how . . . And he said to me: "Now Copel are you gone nuts?! Did I ever give you any sign I'm mad at you? Did I turn My face from you? Do you know yourself to be at fault with Me? Really, Copel, enough of this non-sense, you do know *My Son also became a Christian!*"'

Itzak yelped and Rabbi Copel felt the old man was about to faint. So he slapped him thoroughly. Then he gave him a glass of water. Itzak drank it up thirstily.

'Now run along, Itzak, and prepare the Sabbath in good peace. And tell David to go make a living in a different town. Go now. And be sure to call me to bless your grandchildren when the time comes.'

***

Stiff as a broomstick, Itzak closed behind him the gate to the rabbi's house.

He looked at his kin as if he was seeing them for the first time. He took off his hat and wiped his forehead with the back of his sleeve.

He thought of his pastry and *braga* business.

Then finally he shook his head and walked back home to a new Sabbath.

CHAPTER 4

For a Christian, truthfully living into God means:
moderation – which is generosity
wisdom – which is meekness
power – which is sacrifice
humility – which is the art and science of leading.
The order can be different. Who knows?
But can a man be like this?
Can a Christian be like this?
Can even a part of all these make a good Christian?
Being a Man, Jesus Christ was so much more.

(Theophil Magus)

A WRITER'S TALE

Once upon a time there was a writer. He lived in this wide world of ours as one whose only gift was to write books. The kind of books, however, which from the first to the last page are pure fantasy, no more than tales spun by the human mind to talk of who men are and what they do, and about how they have done good deeds and evil deeds since Adam walked the earth.

And this writer, who had a family, friends and foes, like everyone else, had sailed successfully half way through his life and had written quite a few books, when it dawned on him that he cannot live another day without finding for himself the answer to a question that had been besetting him for a while now.

He knew only to well that this question had tormented many other writers more or less famous than himself, just as he knew that none of them, had they even been his parent or brother, would have shared with him the true answer. For this is how things work between writers and generally between people.

So this writer kept wondering, if I write books that are pleasing for everyone and everywhere, equally read by friend and by foe, I will make good and useful money. I will no longer have to worry about tomorrow. Even more, I will enjoy fame and countless favors. And if I write those wonderful and wise books that I hold so dear to my heart, few will buy them and fewer still read them, while the money will be less than I need to keep myself from starving. To say nothing of my family. I can't be happy if I'm rich. I can't be happy if I'm poor.

Which path should I choose? Thus our writer kept torturing himself day and night as he strove to find the right answer.

Finally he gave up writing books entirely. Both the ones that please everyone everywhere, and the ones full of beauty and wisdom, that he held so dear.

He kept himself busy for a few years gardening, teaching grammar lessons to those who needed that kind of thing, and spending the money he had made from selling his books so that at least his wife and children may live a carefree life.

He would tell all, even his family, the same lie: 'I'm writing the book of my life and this story keeps me busy all the time.'

Naturally, that was not what was really happening.

All the writer did all this time was ask himself the same old question over and over again in various forms. Over and over again.

The man was utterly unhappy. He was running out of money and his palms were itching with the desire to write again. Any book.

Yet he wanted to know what was best and what was the right choice to make.

What finally happened was what one expects will happen to such writers under such circumstances.

Everyone abandoned him. Even his family.

God alone did not abandon him. Our man found a modest job and started his life over again, living the simple and natural life of an ordinary fellow.

After a while, he forgot all about his question. But one night he dreamt that he was talking to this other man, a man whose face he could not see. He knew he was a writer like himself. The man told him: 'You eat when you are hungry, you drink when you are thirsty, you sleep when you are tired. Write, then, just as you manage to do all these other things. It is really that simple. Live as you breathe. Write as you breathe. It is really that simple.'

In the morning, the man woke up, gave a long yawn, stretched his bones till they snapped. Then he washed, ate something for he felt hungry, drank his coffee, and smoked a cigarette. For that's what he felt like doing. And when he finished all that, leaving aside all senseless questions and answers, he started writing.

His first true book.

THE TALE OF THE ROMANIANS

The Book of the Truth about the Nations of the Earth reads as follows:

"Between the waters of the Danube and the Carpathian Mountains, God ordained a country with fertile fields, lavish hills, woody mountains, rivers and lakes teeming with fish, forests that harbor many creatures. He also decreed rain and snow, as well as lots of sun, and spring, and summer, and fall, and winter. In his love, God poured his bounty between the Danube and the Carpathians.

Then God made the Romanian healthy, strong, smart, and industrious. He also gave him many skills that he may find comfort in his mortal life.

Then He made the Romanian the master of the country between the Danube and the Carpathians.

For a while, God left the Romanian to slowly get used to his country and leisurely multiply.

Then God sent for the Romanian and told him:

'Before you set out to make the life of your people in centuries to come, for as long as this world will last, you may ask three things of Me. They will be the boon of your persistence and that of your people. But beware! These three wishes will forever distinguish you from other people. Thus I have spoken and so it shall be.'

The Romanian asked God to give him some time to talk it over with his people.

And God granted him the respite between two springs.

At the end of this term, the Romanian came to God and spoke thus:

'Lord, this is what we have decided:

Let the Romanian never covet the goat of his neighbor.

Wherever he may chance to live in this world, let the Romanian never forsake a fellow Romanian or his country, no matter how hard it may be for him.

Let the Romanian increase Your bounteous gifts, Lord.

God looked down to the Romanian and said:

'Let it be so. But see that you and your people honor me with your heart, not merely with your lips.'

The Romanian thanked God and left to join his people.

On his return to his rich country, between the Danube and the Carpathians, and to his healthy, strong, smart, and industrious people, just as God had ordained it, he spoke to those gathered to hear God's will:

'Let us rejoice, for our wish has been granted!'

'We thank you, Lord!' answered the Romanian people.

Then they started celebrating in great mirth.

And when enough wine had flowed, the Romanians confessed to one another that *any miracle lasts for only three days.*

God heard them and granted them the three wishes of their Romanian will.

And thus distinguished them forever from the rest of the people of the Earth."

THE TALE OF THE POPE AND THE RABBI

Time is a present running endlessly ahead and behind, behind and ahead and only the One eternal all encompassing, omniscient and omnipotent Lord knows why people are the way they are and can hardly understand each other.

This tale tells of the time when people everywhere were looking towards reconciliation, which, as always, was almost impossible.

It was the year 2050.

The Apocalypse of mankind is one (naturally, there are now several Apocalypses, weighing as much as a tooth ache, or animal rights, or the eradication of cancer etc.), yes-yes, a single and tremendously important one: how to reconcile the Christians and the Jews – and do they have a single God, a single Redeemer? (For the Buddhists were mild and impartial, the Muslim quibbled eternally over the rights to Mohammed, and Allah was just another name for God anyway – as for the rest, they were but swarming particles turning aimlessly left, then right, oh, and yes, definitely, the Hindu, yes, nice people, no special demands, as are the Taoists, in fact . . . well, there you are . . .)

The year 2050, then.

And world tension had risen to an unbearable pitch.

The great world powers decide to have a summit meeting. Yes, of course, and who was to meet?

Well, the Pope and the Rabbi.

At hearing the news, the nations of the world became restless and frantic, verging on madness – internationally. Already as many as the sand of the seas, people thought:

'There, the hour of the Apocalypse is come; it's now or never! It must be now or there will be no standing stone left in the world!'

And all – absolutely all thought like that, for, you see, the Christians and the Jews held the knife and the bread . . .

Well, at last, they decided to have the meeting on Easter Island. Many were relieved, for, there you have it, they had chosen a common and somewhat neutral name and place. They both celebrated and made merry at Easter time.

The big planetary event was called 'Anno Domini', and why not? It had been so perfectly organized that everything was paid by donations and sponsorships, naturally with the expected modest advertising.

Well, the day came at last, with a capital, gigantic D.

A non-specific, neutral date in the calendar. They had carefully seen to that.

The whole world was overwhelmed with one indescribable passion, one single vibration, one fantastic tension.

So many people had gathered on the island, that the more nervous started worrying that the patch of land might sink into the ocean.

Every inhabitant of the Earth, nay, of the Universe, could watch it. It was broadcast across the planet. Platinum disks had been prepared to record the meeting in all known languages, a billion-copy bestseller.

Well, there they were:

The Pope and the Rabbi. Alone in front of the remote control cameras in a room like the cell of a desert hermit.

The Pope – as we've always known him to be. Venerable and wise.

The Rabbi – as we've always known him to be. Wise and venerable.

The Pope says something. The Rabbi also says something.

A stupefying moment. They speak different languages, of course. The Pope tries again. The Rabbi does, too. The same result. Suddenly, they start talking at the same time. Useless.

Silence falls and the entire planet gasps and awaits tremulously. Seismographs register the quaking. Low on the scale, fortunately.

Well, the two men finally smile. They both make the same gesture, at the exact same time: appeasing, mitigating, arms and palms wide open. O.K.: the primordial language, then, gesturing.

After inviting each other for a while, finally it is the Pope who starts, for reasons known by the two men alone.

The Pope raises three fingers of his right hand. The Rabbi immediately responds by raising his index. The Pope makes a wide gesture with his hands drawing a sphere. The Rabbi taps the table with his index. The Pope sighs, picks up a loaf of bread with one hand and a chalice of red wine with the other. The Rabbi smiles and holds out an apple in his open palm.

Silence again. You could hear a fly buzz across the whole planet.

Well, the Pope goes and shouts in Latin:

'I have seen the light! Let there be peace among us! Peace be with you all! Peace be with the Earth!'

For a few moments everyone is dumb with amazement. Then start the cheers, and the laughing and the crying, and then the cheers again from the whole of mankind. It was as if an unknown electric current ran through the whole of mankind and, naturally, the broadcast is ended. After all, once this epoch-making message has been delivered, who is left to watch the screens, big or small, who cares about the Pope or the Rabbi?

And still . . .

And still, like mutant piranhas, that is, driven mad by the smell of blood not only in the water, but also in the air, on the ground, in the cosmic void, everywhere, literally everywhere, the journalists felt it . . . they felt it and flung themselves savagely at the subject once again . . .

The Pope is surrounded from all sides. The questions bite at him, the microphones stab him, the cameras suck his picture. The Rabbi fares no better, he cannot escape. And where is one to hide on that small island, crowded as it is and ready to sink under the weight of so many people?

Eventually, the Pope points his rod at the heavens and shouts with authority, though slightly hysterical:

'Enough! Quiet !!!'

So there is finally silence. What happened, every mouth mutely inquires?

'Well, I showed the Rabbi three fingers – the Holy Trinity, right? He showed me one finger – there is only one God. Fair enough. Then I gestured to him that God is everywhere in the Universe. He cut me short: God is here, with us, now. Fair enough. Then I presented to him the Holy Eucharist, the Mystery of Mysteries, communing of our Lord's body and blood. The Rabbi was prompt to reply. He presented to us the symbol of the original sin and the lost Paradise. Fair enough. So, there you have it, my sons and daughters, there is Peace on Earth! Fair enough.'

At the core of another whirlpool of mutant piranhas, the Rabbi is speaking calmly, with a magic smile:

'Oy, my children, what is there not to understand? The Pope's first mime I answered simply: there aren't three ways, how can there be three ways? There is only one way, just one. Then, to the second mime: why take all the time in the world to solve this problem? Let's do it now, there's plenty more to be done!

Then the third was really simple: he offered me his lunch, I offered him mine and before I could tell what happened, it all ended – well. There you have it, reconciliation, peace, everything is all right.'

Instantly, the journalists spread the words of the two venerable wise men in all four horizons of this world. And the Earth shines with joy. On the crowded island, they all embrace and rejoice in the 'Carnival 2050' which spontaneously infects the whole of mankind, later to be held every second year for who knows how long, maybe more than 2050 years!

In any case, starting with the year 2050, global peace is ensured for at least another 2050 years. At least, statistics would have it that way. Small apocalypses, like toothaches, the eradication of cancer, and animal rights will gradually and naturally find a solution.

By themselves.

THE TALE OF THE WITCH

A sun-soaked October day. Green grass all around. I see green, I hear green, I taste green, I smell green, I touch green, the grass is me all around. I climb the hills and fill the fields and I don't seem to have an end.

I'm so old. Actually, I am ageless.

The sparkling blue. I lie on my back, my thoughts resting in the fresh haystack. There, the grayish locks of the azure envelop me and I am a small cloud floating above, drifting ever farther, somewhere, possibly to the end of the world.

I'm so old. Actually, I am ageless.

I look sideways. A butterfly. Is it real? Black velvet wings stained with rust. The quivering air. What are you doing here now?

I'm so old. Actually, I am ageless.

I close my eyes. I can travel through times. And I stop for a few moments in front of a black king. The words: soft, harsh sounds. Whispered and broken. The weeping of trumpets and saxophones. And I could be by his side as he dies. Only twentysix years old. His name was Otis Redding. A king . . .

I'm so old. Actually, I am ageless.

The hills smile sadly. I smile back faintly. They are slow creatures. Gentle. It's a beautiful day. And the sun. And torn, deeply cut by the autumn, the creatures suffer less. The pride of the superb wounds. And the gentle creatures know it. And on the trees the blood, now matte, now glossy; now live coals, now saffron; now brass, now burnt clay; now neither myself nor someone else could try it without the risk of being intoxicated with unnamable colors. Sad things I sadly smile to myself.

I'm so old. Actually, I am ageless.

Today, too, today, too, I lie on my back and seem not to be breathing. Liquid the silence and the peace. I may be in a glass cage. Today, too, today, too, I seem not to be breathing. What are you looking for?

I'm so old. Actually, I am ageless.

I stand up. Slowly breaking up each move. Grace, fatigue, I no longer know. I walk and shut my eyelids tightly. I have no space. I once more leave the green the sparkling blue the slow creatures and I sing the blues on the black velvet stained with rust.

I'm so old. Actually, I am ageless.

I stop amid the thousands of corpses, amid the armors slashed open and stained purple; I give myself to the fixed glassy stares, the claws clutching the handles of swords and spears, at my feet the numberless heads, portraits carved in hatred despair terror, which only they knew as they rolled away from the bodies; and I cannot mount the steeds with their legs stretched stiff or cringing with a last broken gallop. I am not far from the haystack that offered me a glass cage.

I'm so beautiful. I am so young.

Actually, I am ageless. A signal: as in a dream of the deep waters, the heads find their vassal bodies, the fingers come alive on the handles of the swords and the

spears, the blood seeps back in through the split armor, and the metal regains its luster, the feathers quiver slightly in the breeze, the flags slowly rise, the shouting and the roaring grows, the steeds turn and stand on their hind legs, neighing . . .

I'm so beautiful. I am so young.

Actually, I'm a witch.

A TALE OF SAINT ANTHONY OF PADUA

Once upon a time, in an age about which we know very little, there lived a Franciscan monk called Anthony. And this man was so good, just, merciful, loving, and faithful, that Lord Jesus Christ nestled in his arms as a child and bestowed the cross of chastity on Anthony. And Anthony bore his cross through life, so that men loved and blessed him ever after.

Many are the tales of the wonders, the well doings, and the chaste life of Saint Anthony of Padua, for Padua was the land he cherished the most.

But there is also another tale, less known.

According to it, Saint Anthony hid in the small hermitage of Campo San Pietro, in Padua, as he became tired of the world, the wonders and the healing, the sermons and the heathen he brought to God's ways. He was also bodily sick with the discomforts of his long pilgrimages during which he had no more than his cloak.

He craved for a place to find rest from his doubts, comfort for his soul and peace, and maybe to heal himself.

Few days after he came to that shrine, a weary traveler knocked on the gate. Judging by his appearance, his clothes and his speech, he seemed to be a man of the mountains, a shepherd. Saint Anthony welcomed him lovingly and shared with him everything he owned.

The next morning, having waited for Saint Anthony to finish his prayer, the man spoke:

'May God repay you for the way you welcomed and treated me without asking me anything. Give and you shall receive.

Now here is my gift. Like you, I was rich once and have become poor for the love of God. I have lived in justice, kindness, and charity, and I have loved Jesus. His word made me rich every moment, every hour, and every day. I believe I am one of the wealthiest paupers in this world. Nor do I expect any worldly reward. Word has it you are a man of God. I've come a long way and I humbly ask you to end my torment: tell me if I have really done right all my life, why am I so sick of this world, whence the disgust that overwhelms my soul? What have I misunderstood in God's word, what do I lack?'

'Courage', Anthony whispered unawares. And he hardly noticed when the traveler was off.

***

Months had gone by since the traveler was Saint Anthony's guest.

And Anthony had left the little hermitage and built himself a hut not far from it, in the hollow of a giant oak, by the clear brook, deep in the woods. There he spent almost every hour of the day fasting, praying, and searching.

For he had spoken that word in truth but had no idea why, what its true meaning was.

And first his mind, then his soul and heart had been terribly and variously tempted not by one, but by legions of devils, one for each of the ten commandments, and all punishing him for the cross God had offered him. And Satan rose everywhere, day and night, from the sky, from the water, from the earth.

The day came, though, when, under the blue heavens, there in the green woods, not far from the little hermitage, mirrored by the clear water as he sat in his tree hollow, leaning on his old stick, staring hard within his soul, and free from temptations and impurity – the day came when Saint Anthony slowly and softly spoke:

'Give me, O Lord, the courage to live forever and suffer and heal the pain of this world. Give me, O Lord, the courage to smile when I understand. Give me, O Lord, the courage to enjoy healing.

Give me, O Lord, the courage to carry your gift. Amen.'

Then everything around him became a place for resting, for comfort, and for peace, there in the green old woods, by the clear brook, under the blue heavens. And Saint Anthony sighed with relief. Then he breathed his last.

And God granted him his wish.

CHAPTER 5

Old age without youth and death without life
this would be my existence without my Lord Jesus Christ.

(Theophil Magus)

THE TALE OF A TIGER

Buddha was meditating under a fig tree. The sun had set. The dusk cast shadows that stretched slowly. The jungle was coming alive as it felt the cold breath of the night. The wild creatures were preparing to kill or fight for their lives. The wheel of destiny was turning.

The tiger stopped in front of Buddha and nervously whipped his tail against his hips. It gave out a muffled growl.

Buddha never flinched.

His lids stayed down and his lips remained sealed.

After a while, the tiger lied down in the dry grass under the fig tree, growled lightly, and vented his supplication:

'O Siddhartha, Thou Knower of the Truth, O Enlightened one, please listen to me and give me an answer.'

None but the voices of the jungle were heard, but the tiger understood he could go on:

'A lumberjack was chased by a panther and fell over the edge of a precipice. In his fall, the man grabbed at some wild vine creepers. I heard the roar of the panther and the cries of the man. I was in the bushes below. I saw the panther looking over the edge. It was rabid for losing its prey. The man knew, as did I, what a panther can do when it loses its prey. So the man could not climb up to the edge. At that very moment, two mice started nibbling at the creepers just above the unfortunate lumberjack. I sat quietly below waiting for the prey to fall. Suddenly, though, the man started. I looked closer. It wasn't that high above me. I saw the man staring at a purple berry, the color of hot blood drops, which grew in a crack beside him. He gave it a long stare, then started swinging. When he got close enough he picked the berry, put it in his mouth, then grabbed his creeper again and stood still. I wondered if he would be able to hang there long enough for the mice to cut the creeper loose. But the man turned his head and looked right into my eyes. At first he was terrified, but then he became quiet, serene even. It seemed like an eternity. And suddenly there was that high pitched, piercing cry, as if a thousand peacocks cried at the same time. Oh, Siddhartha, believe me, I barely had time to duck for my life . . . The man had jumped on me . . . Yes, I fled like a scared kitten into the bushes . . . Eventually, I stopped. And I felt rage: the wretched lumberjack was supposed to be my prey. I dashed back, but it was too late. The man had vanished. I observed his marks, smelled the blood trail, the man had hurt himself badly as he fell, so he could not be far. But, O Wise One, I could not move . . . I felt a terror I, the tiger, had never felt before . . . O Buddha, am I still *the tiger*?'

His lids still down, his lips still sealed, Buddha replied:

'You are what you are and the jungle still trembles in front of you. But now you will be the man who was supposed to be your prey.'

Thus, the tiger found itself hanging above the abyss, desperately clutching the creepers. The panther above, the tiger below. And the mice . . .

***

The moon was weaving its light under the fig tree. Just as still and impenetrable, Buddha asked the tiger:

'How did that feel?'

'O Siddhartha, I have met *the tiger*, but the wonderful taste of the berry . . .'

OLD TALE

The tribe had never hunted better than at the foot of that mountain, never found more fish than in that clear and whirling river, never picked more wild fruit. So they stayed on for the whole summer and fall as well. A long and serene fall.

Winter drew near and some of the elders said the rich game, fish, and fruits, the beautiful summer and fall, all pointed to a hard winter. But they had lingered too long at the foot of the mountain and there was not enough time to return to the lands of milder winters.

They held council and having carefully considered their situation, they sent one of the hunters to the hermit that lived in a cave above the rain clouds. The envoy was to ask the wise old man what the winter was going to be like and how the tribe should prepare for it.

The hunter took the offerings and left at the break of day.

By sundown he had reached the hermit.

He bowed, presented the offerings, and asked. The wise old man gave him a searching look and replied:

'It will be a winter. Prepare well.'

***

The hunter slept over in the hermit's cave and headed back for his tribe at the break of day.

He arrived before sundown and brought back the answer.

They worked hard to prepare themselves, they dried and smoked the meat and the fish, they picked fruit and healing roots and herbs, they gathered fire wood, they mended their tents, choosing the warmest skins and furs, and they built shelters for the horses.

As soon as the elders, the chief, and the more respected men thought they had done what was needed, the council decided to send the hunter again to see the wise hermit.

The man found himself once more at the cave entrance, bowed, placed the offerings on the mossy rock, and asked. The wise old man gave him a long look and said:

'It will be a hard winter. Prepare well.'

The tribe worked even harder.

Days went by. The council met once more and once again sent the hunter. The gentle but penetrating voice of the old man was heard once more:

'It will be a very hard winter! Prepare well!'

They labored like ants. Each one praised the Lord above for the hermit living up there in the cave.

Days went by and when the council met again, they decided that this time they must send none other than the chief himself.

***

As he stood at the cave entrance, the worthy man bowed, humbly presented the offerings and spoke:

'O wisest of men, each time we took your advice and prepared for this winter as never before. O wisest of men, we are so well prepared that our elders believe we are ready for two long winters. Tell us, I pray you, how hard will this winter be?'

The old man gave him a long look and finally spoke softly but clearly:

'It will be unimaginably hard. Prepare well.'

Awestruck, the man took a step back. He struggled to conquer his trembling. After a long while, he ventured in a coarse voice:

'O wisest of men, forgive my boldness, but why is it that each time we asked for your advice you foretold this winter to be harder and harder, and now you say it is going to be unimaginably hard?'

The old man gave him a long look and answered abruptly:

'Come.'

The chief followed him to the edge of the cliff. The air was crystal clear and the worthy man could see his tribe. He saw the woodpiles and the men busy as ants.

The hermit laid his hand on the man's shoulder:

'There, you see them? They have been preparing for this winter like nobody ever did before them. It will be an unimaginably hard winter', the old man severely decided, then returned to his cave above the rain clouds and the snow clouds . . . Who knows ? . . .

A TALE ABOUT THE EXACT TIME

It *once happened like this:*

The man opened his eyes, yawned, and looked, as he did each morning, to the curtainless window. Outside floated that typical winter-dawn dimness. His eyes on the frozen window, the man picked up the phone, put it to his ear, and mechanically dialed the number. He waited a while, then moved his lips:

'Good morning – the Institute for measurements? Could you please tell me the exact time?'

He listened, ready to thank and set his alarm clock and wristwatch. But the man at the other end said:

'Hello, please don't hang up. This time, could you please answer our question?'

'Yes', he replied, although surprised by the breech of protocol, always the same these many past years.

'We've never declined to assist you . . . but could you please at least tell us who you are? Your voice, we can already easily recognize it . . .'

'I'm just another guy working at the factory next to your institute. I was told you are the most qualified to give me the exact time. For years now I've been in charge to signal the beginning and the end of the workday by blowing the siren. Now can I have the exact time?'

There was a muffled noise of surprise at the other end.

'Is something wrong?'

'O no, no . . . How shall I put this? . . . You see, for years now we have been setting our clocks by your factory siren . . .'

The man became restless for not having set his watch and running out of time to get to his siren. He was a bit irritated as he replied:

'Fine, whatever, but can I please have the exact time? We forgot the time chatting and I have a job to do, I have responsibilities, please . . .'

It once happened.

DONOLIVIU'S TALE

In the year of 1998, as always at the beginning of spring, the crowds were frenetic and swarming like ants in *1 May* marketplace in one of the great districts of Bucharest. The teeming sellers and buyers constantly chattered and gesticulated. The stands were loaded with things that brought quick and sure profits, on top, underneath, and on side-racks there were fruits, big boxes, little boxes, bottles of different sizes, all sorts of jars, bags, oil, tomato paste, mustard, jams, preserves, sugar, rice, soap, detergent, matches, stockings, toys, cigarettes, and what-not. If you had the money . . .

Everyday, it is easy to understand, madness broke loose in the marketplace. Housewives, spouses in couples or alone, pensioners, children, peasants from the countryside or from the city, merchants and sellers, beggars and homeless people, policemen, tax men, stray cats and dogs, a real Babel. Deals, arguments, politics and football, gossip and scandals, horns hooting, engines roaring, loud gypsy and disco music – a singular sonorous and fascinating inferno.

But enough of that. The reason I told you all these things is to make you understand that none of us can resist the magnet of the seething marketplace. You may love it, or hate it. Or you may simply need it. Or all of that at once.

Also, I had to go through all this, to make you understand that DonOliviu was crazy about this kind of life. Especially because his parents and the dear Lord had made him short, fat, lively, cuddly, with restless green eyes under the tuft of tobacco hair, lips constantly torn between an ill-contained laughter and an unquenched appetite. He was made to look like a spoiled child even though he was forty, a child everyone loved for his pranks and his good nature, for his quick, stubby hands, and for his cheerful penguin walk.

DonOliviu, yes he was and still is a math teacher. But DonOliviu wanted – and it was only natural in a country where math teachers earned barely enough to pay their rent and buy cigarettes – he craved for a life in the marketplace. He nevertheless hired someone to man the stand for he still loved to teach the kids numbers, equations, roots, which meant he had to be in class every day.

But at the end of the school day DonOliviu would climb into his little, dirty, battered red automobile and rather than stop home to see his wife first, he would go straight to his marketplace stand. Here he spent hours on end with his seller, helping him, supervising him, but most of all chatting with the people.

They all knew him and liked him in the *1 May* marketplace and someone was bound to call out 'Teacher!' on a ten-meter radius around his stand. And this nickname had nothing to do with his being a math teacher, rather with his pleasure, this thing he had – to ask market people and clients strange questions.

'What is the *smaller* infinite?' 'Have you ever been *un*happy?' Who are we, where do we come from, and where are we *not* going?' 'Is a *smaller* zero times a *greater* zero still a zero?' 'What is the difference between a dead dog and a live lion?' or 'Why did God send us away from Heaven if He made us in His own likeness and after His image?' and other such creations from the Teacher.

Obviously, there were as many answers as there were people he would ask. And DonOliviu would laugh merrily, argue with a smile, offer small prizes, an orange, a chocolate, or discount delicatessen. One thing he was sure of, though, he would never receive the expected answer, or an answer he would not be able to complete, leaving his interlocutor speechless.

Life went on like this and DonOliviu did not feel himself growing old, the little Socrates of the *1 May* marketplace.

But one morning he woke up in a bad mood. Nothing could relax his frowning face, not even a delicious cabbage salad with a pile of fries soaked in the juice of a rich cutlet. You got it, nothing worked. For DonOliviu had learned that the Teacher lacked a question that would send even him thinking. Yes, yes, the question he would not be able to answer.

***

And so it was that the lovely early spring and the *1 May* marketplace had been beset for over a month by the same obsessive question: 'Ask and you shall be given. Seek and you shall find. Knock and you shall be answered. What do you think Jesus meant by that?' And the Teacher sighed with relief once he asked that question and then smiled amiably.

Nobody tried to avoid the question and each gave their own explanation, according to their knowledge, their abilities, and their beliefs.

Many took DonOliviu to be part of a cult, but he patiently persuaded them that he was neither an atheist, nor a cult member, he was just another Christian who wanted to understand these words of God.

But, as time went by, DonOliviu became ever more sullen. Even though some provided full-blown lectures, priests, philosophers, sociologists, Jehovah's witnesses. Even though a few peasants gave him simple, well-behaved, wise answers, DonOliviu knew he had not yet received the answer he was waiting for.

In short, DonOliviu came down ill. He pined, he could not sleep well, his appetite was gone, he ached . . .

For he himself could not answer the question.

***

Sometime, at the beginning of the Lent, a little rogue from the neighborhood stopped in front of his stand. The kid listened to DonOliviu's conversation with a pensioner about the obsessive question, then he spoke:

'Hey, mister, I know that one. Honest.'

'Nah', DonOliviu said distrustful.

'But you'll have to give me an orange . . .'

'O so you just want the orange . . .'

'No, I don't. Honestly, mister, but since I'm gonna give you the answer there ought to be something in it for me too.'

'Here's your orange.'

The kid snatched it and ran off. Teacher had a hearty laugh. So did all around him.

***

Three days later the kid came back but would not get anywhere near the stand. DonOliviu saw him and shouted:

'Hey, you! Come on over. I won't do anything to you . . . Come on, look I'll give you some chocolate. Or an orange, whichever you choose. Come on now!'

The kid drew near. He wasn't really afraid but he was cautious.

'Mister . . .'

DonOliviu gestured him down abruptly. Then he asked the question. The kid buckled up like a young goat ready to charge, then he ran his dirty fingers through his golden locks, and his black eyes caught fire. Finally he exposed his weasel teeth and replied quickly and firmly:

'I don't feel like it. I'll tell you tomorrow though. So, do I get anything?'

DonOliviu gave him a bar of chocolate. He wasn't really sure why.

***

They played the same little game every day for a week.

Something was happening though. And the people started noticing that DonOliviu was becoming his old self again: the nice, good-natured, merry Teacher. DonOliviu was still a little sad. And confused. And uncomforted for not knowing the answer himself. A voice inside him, though, told him the little rogue, the young comedian who managed to get under his skin, yes even this child knew it. And DonOliviu was waiting for it every day. He only found peace when he saw the child.

***

The kid stopped in front of the stand. He was slightly rocking on his feet, making ready for the usual, yet each time different confrontation, filling him with the excitement of a child's soul.

DonOliviu brightened up as soon as he saw the child in the distance. Just as excited, though, he said:

'Welcome! And thank you for the answer.'

The kid's eyes opened wide.

Then he pouted.

Good bye oranges, chocolate, bananas, he thought with a heavy heart.

'What's the matter? No, honestly, you did give me my answer.'

The child almost burst into tears.

He looked straight into the Teacher's eyes.

His face, like a full moon after the rain calmed his racing heart.

He felt a dim yet overwhelming joy and burst into a loud laughter that sounding through the marketplace.

This made DonOliviu happy to.

The market people and the buyers all stopped still for a second, confused, wondering, then they resumed their daily turmoil and the noise swallowed the happy laughter.

'Now you listen here carefully', the Teacher ordered the boy. 'You will come here and collect your prize as usual even when I'm not around.

Don't get greedy on me or you'll make me broke.'

The child took his orange and a chocolate and was off to his child life business.

And ever since, the Teacher never asked people questions unless they could be answered by a child.

OUR TALE

The Heaven and the Earth shall pass, but My words shall not pass . . .

. . . Thomas spoke slowly, clearly and crisply, there, in the Bengal Gulf, and it was as if the sunset pulsed with a white-golden light, and the sand swished long and silky; the ocean waves themselves seemed to beat the shores in silence.

The jungle nearby gave a short murmur, then fell silent too, as if with a new, unknown, and mild comfort.

Thomas stood there for a while, head raised at the heavens, eyes shut, lips half-open, erect and with his arms open wide.

He prayed silently for the Word of his Lord and Master. He prayed passionately, yet trustful and humble. For, he was at the gates of the great India, with its countless people of whom he knew almost nothing.

And he alone had been chosen to share the Gospel with them. All he had on him was the Holy Ghost, a long linen shirt and a cedar wood walking stick. In his goatskin bag he kept enclosed in a sycamore box the scroll on which God had asked him to mark down His words.

The night before, one of God's Angels came to him in a dream. It commanded him to come to this place at this time of the day. He was to meet the three Magi from the East who worshipped the Infant and offered him gold, incense and myrrh in that holy hour in Bethlehem. They would put him to the test and he would be victorious. Then he, Thomas, was to baptize them, and the Magi were to assist him in the work that God commanded of him there, in the great and unknown India.

Though the prayer had filled his heart and mind with serenity, comfort, and hope, Thomas quivered with fear as he sat waiting on the warm sand. 'I am still human', he admitted.

***

'Awake', said a voice inside Thomas, as if God were by his side.

He started and opened his eyes wide.

It was dusk.

He saw the camp, the fretting servants, the fires and the tents.

The horses gave subdued neighs, the kneeling camels snorted.

'May the Angels watch over you, may God protect you, may Jesus guide your heart', the deep whisper sounded in the break of night.

Thomas gave thanks by crossing himself and it was then that he saw the three Magi, Gaspar, Balthazar, and Melhior, standing in a circle . . .

The Magi looked like ageless old people, and they smiled gently, as their eyes cast secret sparkles like the celebrated gems of India.

'Thank you for coming. I await and honor your wisdom', Thomas said.

'Thomas', Melhior spoke for the Magi, 'the Word is everywhere and it is alive.

In Bethany you said: "Let us go and die with Him!" And you received Word: "I am the Resurrection and the life." At the Easter Supper you said: "Lord, we know not whither you are gone; how may we learn the way?" And you received Word: "I am the way, the truth, and the life. None shall come to the Father but by Me."

Then, what is the truth you are hiding, Thomas?'

Thomas breathed, seized by an unseen fire, then slowly, slowly he came to himself. The Holy Ghost filled him completely. His eyes opened wide, wide – and when he finally saw Him, he spoke:

'O My Lord and Master, if this be Your wish, I witness the cross you gave me.'

Unflinching in their gentle smiles, their eyes glowing, palms pressed to their hearts, the Eastern Magi listened. And it seemed like the heaven and the earth passed at that very moment.

'Behold, O Lord, what was, and You know well that thus it all came to pass. You rose, O Lord, for You died on the cross. And they all learned it. Jerusalem was up on its feet. The Sadducees and the Pharisees went mad. And I, Thomas, pure and humble and faithful as you had found me in Lazarus' Bethany, and whom You anointed with Your Word at that Last Supper on Easter Day, I knew from You that it was to be like that. For I was commanded by You to preserve Your Words in eternity. Amen.

'And remember, O Lord, when I saw the countenance of Mary Magdalene come out of the house where my brethren were hiding, I knew Your promise was true that You shall never suffer us to become orphans. I was speechless with joy. Yet I went in. I saw my brethren. I saw with my heart the inside of their hearts.

'And then I asked: Lord, I happily take upon myself their sin, as You did to redeem us. Lord, help their lack of faith and come back into your frame of flesh that I may thrust my finger into their unfaithfulness and Your wounds, saving them, for they loved You best and shall witness with their lives their love for You.

'Happily I say: Lord, may my name be Doubting Thomas, in eternity and until I shall pass from this world, if that may help me love my brethren as my self. Help me, my Lord and Master, teach me.'

Then fell silent Thomas, alias the Twin, alias the Doubting.

Melhior spoke for the Magi:

'Let it be ours, the story of your brethren, let it be our story.

Baptize us, Thomas.'

And Doubting Thomas baptized them.

In the name of our Lord.

With water of the Indian Ocean and with the Holy Spirit.

CHAPTER 6

At the start of this 21st century,
looking around me, but also at myself, I had to admit,
to recognize with bitterness,
that after two thousand years of Christianity
there are not too many people who have real shadows.
Lord Jesus Christ sighs:
"If therefore the light that is in you is darkness,
how great is that darkness!"

(Theophil Magus)

A TALE ABOUT TWO OLD PEOPLE

She came into the room and sat in her armchair. She sighed softly and carefully straightened her dress over her knees. He heard her, put down his book on the nearby table, rose from his own armchair (they had tacitly agreed the one with the wood carved arms and blue velvet rest is his), lit a cigarette and went to her *what's the matter?* And his dried-out fingers, the index and the middle finger stained by the yellow tobacco, rested with a quiver on her shoulder bones. *Nothing, I'm thinking of cooking vine-leaf rolls, should I grind the meat or shall we eat kosher? What's the matter, Brigitte?* They looked each other in the eyes – the last sparkles inhabiting the desert, *what are you reading, Nardi? A book about extinct animals – like ourselves . . . never mind, what is the matter? Well . . . I had a dream . . . Go ahead and tell me about it, Brigitte, And give me a cigarette too. Here,* she lit one, the smoke coiling up from their pink-blue lips, *O, Nardi, such a weird dream . . . I could smell my body, it was very hot and I was sweating, I could feel my armpits all wet . . . I was in our old flat, you were all out, the kids and all, I was thinking about you, but there was this great sadness, and my body somehow smelled like a corpse, I was wondering how we managed to survive all this time together, you, me, and the kids, and I kept seeing in front of me a dark rock covered with moss . . . I went for a shower and when I came back the room smelled fresh . . . but the bitter sadness was still haunting me and I looked at the sun and it made me blind . . . I was so scared in the dark, I knew someone was preparing to deal me a pitiless blow, the terror made me see again and there was this deep silence in the room . . . I felt like I was floating, I grabbed at the curtains suddenly, and squeezed that something which fluttered inside it, funny, I couldn't tell what it was, all I could see were its beautiful transparent wings, and I felt I had to take revenge so I took that creature, clutching my fist, and went to the kitchen, I poured honey on a piece of paper, then dropped the creature in the honey – again I had no idea what it was – and let it toss about, and then I set it on fire, you know Nardi I was fascinated by the way the transparent wings were burning . . . then I found myself on the balcony holding a small heap of ashes in my open palm and wondering why it smelled like burning flesh, I dropped the ashes on the cement and was going back into the room when I heard a moan I turned on my heels and fell to my knees by the burnt woman, her lips, her breasts, her belly cracked by the flames, I threw up, the dying woman opened her eyes and tried to whisper something to me, I put my ear to her lips,*

I heard your name and it suddenly dawned on me I was the burnt, the dying woman, so I jumped from the balcony, except I did not fall but floated in midair watching myself . . . yes, this is what I dreamt, Nardi, o, and another thing, after I flung myself from the balcony and remained suspended, I remember wondering what will I do when you show and find me like that, burnt on the balcony and also suspended, watching myself in terror . . . Brigitte, these are just dreams, what can I tell you . . . just relax now but the old woman started weeping . . .

. . . Nardi took away her cigarette and put it out.

He stroked her head.

Look at me, Brigitte, I ate like a pig last night and slept like a log, and you dreamt this thing . . . Brigitte! he shouted. The old woman wiped her eyes with her hand.

Give me another cigarette, There, Okay, it happened, what do you want?

She lit her cigarette. Silent for a while. Vague thoughts. Broken memories. An occasional exhaling puff. And when their eyes met:

Brigitte: I'll go make those rolls.

Nardi: Forget the damn rolls!

Brigitte: I have to cook, it's almost ten; don't worry, go ahead and read your book. Shall I make you some coffee? Why don't you listen to a CD? How about Mozart?

Nardi: Forget the damn rolls, listen to this, there once were tiger whose fangs were as long as a dagger, that's why they became extinct, they would get stuck in their prey . . .

Brigitte: What if the kids show up for supper?

Nardi: They won't, we stopped calling them, they haven't been here for a month now, they won't be coming.

Brigitte: Maybe they called when we were out, maybe . . .

Nardi: You're not going to start that again? Nobody calls any more, I'm tired of people calling, forget the damn rolls, take a book and sit by my side . . .

Brigitte: When I'm in the kitchen I forget . . .

Nardi: Nonsense, you remember . . .

Brigitte: Nardi . . .

Nardi: Get dressed, we won't be coming back home before tonight.

Brigitte: What will we be doing out?

Nardi: We'll be trying to forget differently, or remember differently. For a moment they stared at each other tensely. Then they smiled embarrassed.

***

They were walking slowly looking at the white roses at the edge of the sidewalk. Brigitte showed him a rose bud with mother-of-pearl petals. Nardi wanted to pluck it. She wouldn't let him, there are people, there's bound to be a moralist around. But we are old, this is our last wish, he laughed. No, it's better this way, I don't feel like dealing with intruders. Fine, whatever you say, and he put his arm around her shoulders. Some of the passers by would turn their heads. Nardi, a bit bald on top, close hair cut, his beard still black only in a couple of places, his Mongol eyes slightly fixed, tallish and chubby, wearing an off-white flax summer suit, Brigitte, flowing copper hair swinging on her frail shoulders, brown, bright, made-up eyes, restless and yet sad, slender in her elegant dark blue velvet overalls – both of them with an elastic, yet vaguely tired strut, their faces serene as if expecting an imminent redemption. *Nardi, tell me something about the book you're reading, What can I say, Brigitte, I think – well, we're over sixty – I think we ought to learn the joy of going back to our childhood books, our childhood curiosity, this book is called On the Trail of Rare and Fabulous Animals . . . Nardi, I remember reading somewhere, actually I know exactly where, but that's beside the point, something about the ambivalence of time, I'd rather call it duality, whatever . . . that duplicity of time where it . . . well, you know the Romanian proverb: 'the hour runs and hits, time is forever'* . . . Nardi laughed faintly, shook his head, *we perish in eternity, right? But how do we perish? This book, true legends, honestly, Brigitte, we are neither rare nor fabulous – and I'm starving* . . . the old lady snorted with amusement, then raised her arm and pointed at the terrace, *now, Nardi, when was the last time we had sausages? And a beer? Yes, my darling.*

They walked into the broad plaza and headed at leisure, past the stream of shoppers, to the sausage-and-beer terrace, back in a more withdrawn corner of the plaza, next to the dormitories of the flatland peasants come to sell their products up here in the mountains. Nardi went to the bar to order while Brigitte sat at a table. She lifted the tablecloth and shook off the crumbs. Then she replaced it and evened it out with the palm of her hand. From the bar Nardi watched her as she lit a cigarette and started to smoke. He felt goose bumps on his skin. He lit a cigarette himself. The rumor of the busy plaza. The smoke and sausage aroma. This world – , he thought, and shrugged. As if he had briskly shaken off an unseen burden.

What can I get you? came the bartender's harsh, hurried voice. Ah, yes, Nardi

came to, ten sausages, well done, if you don't mind, four rolls, mustard, chilly and three beers. And a small vodka. Ice and lemon. How much is it? Sixty-five, sir. Thank you. Thank you, sir. Take a seat and the girl will be right with you. Brigitte clapped her hands in admiration seeing him come back with a broad grin. The girl turned up as soon as Nardi sat at the table.

Brigitte inspected the sausages, smelled them: *o Nardi my mouth is all watery . . . Mine too, an excellent idea, by the way, when was the last time we . . . I really can't remember, Neither can I, but I do remember when it first happened . . . O what does it matter when . . . Still, I will tell you, it already happened now, just as that first time,* they laughed, *Shakespeare,* he said and placed his index on the tip of her nose, *Longfellow,* she replied, put out her index and put on a Laurel grin.

They chewed carefully each bite and occasionally sipped their beer. Each had something to say that made the other smile or lean back and laugh. They looked in each other's eyes trying to open the window to the other's inside. To be able to breathe deeply some fresh air. Gradually, they forgot about the rest of the world and became a little island floating quietly. It did not matter where.

They started. The speakers started bellowing a gypsy ballad. Nardi raised a hand and snapped his fingers in a flourish. Brigitte took her head in her hands and pretended she was crying desperately. Then they started laughing heartily.

The restaurant was invaded by a group of loud youngsters, outrageously dressed and made up. They cared nothing for those around them. Seized with a vague and painful nostalgia, Brigitte and Nardi stopped eating. They lit a cigarette and set off on a pilgrimage towards their long-ago selves, their long-ago children. Two girls noticed them. They said something to the others and the din and the fooling around stopped. The whole group turned and looked at the two old people. Questioning, irritated, contemptuous. No trace of curiosity or anything else . . . Brigitte forced herself to smile to them. She failed. Nardi seized her arm. They put off their cigarettes.

They stood up.

They left. Light, even, calm tread. An uneasy voice inside: old fart!

The gypsy pain humming in the speakers: "O heart of mine . . . "

***

The sun about to bloody its body.

The melting asphalt.

The wind hardly breathing.

Nardi: I have to say I'm a bit tired.

Brigitte: You old fart!

Nardi: Do you remember the bit in the *Jungle Book* cartoon with the bald eagles?

Brigitte: The one where they perch on a branch and start asking one another "so what are we going to do now?" Yes, that was funny, Nardi . . .

Nardi: The stroke of a genius, Disney, he nailed us . . .

Brigitte: Watch out for that child!

Nardi: So what are we going to do now?

Brigitte: I don't know; what do you want to do?

Nardi: Did you see the circus posters?

Brigitte: It's so hot, I'm thirsty . . .

Nardi: We left an almost full beer bottle on the table . . .

Brigitte: Let's go to the circus, maybe they have a polar bear or a lady that plays the trumpet . . .

Nardi: Very well, madam Fellini, let's go to the circus.

Brigitte: Old man, did we use to get bored like this when we were twenty?

Nardi: Except we did not use to think about death.

Brigitte: We don't now, we are dead.

Nardi: So what do you want to do now?

They stopped for a soda in front of a stand. They paid. Then they drank, eyes closed, still holding hands. An old couple slightly bent. With the heat. Or . . .

***

The sleepy afternoon floated above the park.

Two old people.

On a bench.

No one else.

Around.

Not a thing in sight.

No.

The vegetal peace.

No.

A hand.

Dried up fingers.

Endlessly caressing.

A shoulder.

Bony.

No.

The gesture.

And yet the vacuum.

In the numbness of nature, an almost imperceptible voice:

Nardi, my dream . . . was . . . Just a dream, believe me, don't be afraid . . . it's just the two of us, believe me . . .

Nardi raised his head.

As always he unwittingly wondered at the trees' pentagram.

Above the grass there floated a mist and a smell of agonizing summer.

Brigitte, my old lady, the circus is in town, shall we give it a try? Yes, let's, my old gentleman.

***

They managed to find good seats. It must have been that the booth lady liked their faces or sensed the tip that came promptly.

As the show went on, the old couple, shoulder to shoulder, arm in arm, hip to hip, knee to knee, shiver to shiver, became two mesmerized children.

Acrobats on a suspended wire, Icaruses at the trapeze, the horse-riders of Genghis-Khan, the laugh-weep clowns, the musician elephants, jugglers with bottles and balls and plates and knives and torches, jumpers through fire hoops, through terror, panthers, tigers, and lions, and the lips of the two old people tightly shut, or agape, their eyes shut or their pupils dilated, their nostrils sniffing at the danger or at their own fear – Brigitte and Nardi were in no way different from the kids around them, all having stepped together and identical into a fairy-tale.

The long rapping of drums. Then silence – and the hundreds of painfully held breaths. The circus manager in the arena. He greets the public with a short nod. The pause. Brigitte's fingers sneaked into Nardi's. Then clenched them.

'Ladies and gentlemen, esteemed public, we take pride in presenting to you the world premiere of the latest and extraordinary number by the notorious magician Garuda!'

The drums. The manager gestured broadly with his right arm. A man in a green silk tuxedo walked into the arena, his head wrapped in a yellow turban. He greeted the public with a faint bow. His big black beard with bluish streaks in the spotlights. He took the microphone from the manager and spoke with a subtle, yet warm vibrato that spread a sense of confidence throughout the audience:

'Ladies and gentlemen, good evening. Welcome. My number is not extraordinary and is not even a world premiere.' Laughter, the manager himself smiled. 'This magic trick, my own creation, is unique in the world and I have presented it in many performances around the globe. It is simple, fascinating, and not at all dangerous. Many of my magician colleagues envy me for this success. This unique magical number is called "The Vanishing". For the best results, I perform this number on three subjects: the audience and two volunteers from the audience. Each of the two volunteers will vanish to each other, though none of them will actually vanish. You, the audience, are the witness. Shall I repeat? Very well. Who, then, will kindly volunteer?

Nardi whispered to Brigitte, *hypnosis, mere hypnosis, double hypnosis*, she added, *it's not that simple, how is he going to simultaneously induce the vanishing, the same target, in two different directions*, he gestured, *he's got experience after all these shows . . . it'll be fun anyway*, Brigitte smiled, *why don't we try it ourselves?* Nardi turned to her surprised, saw the thrill on her face and went stiff, *oh come on now, it's okay to let ourselves go for once in our lives*, Brigitte giggled like a spoiled brat.

***

Brigitte and Nardi asked Garuda's permission to hold hands. The magician accepted. He did not smile. He just bowed to his audience and respectfully acknowledged his volunteers. He spoke out: 'The Vanishing'. He did not raise his voice. Yet, he was heard by each and every person under the huge circus tent.

Then "the vanishing" followed.

Nardi realized he no longer felt Brigitte's fingers. He blinked confused. It was just him, Garuda, and the audience!

Brigitte realized she no longer felt Nardi's fingers. She blinked confused. It was just her, Garuda, and the audience!

Nardi looked around, then searched among the witness-spectators.

Brigitte looked around, then searched among the witness-spectators.

The silence of the witnesses. The hundreds of eyes. The arena and its fabulous peacock tail. Garuda – they both remembered – the imperial bird, the destroyer of the demon serpents. The hundreds of looks converging on them, on Garuda. The immobility of the magus. Everyone was silent. And they all saw. Petrified.

This silence. This petrifying. This vanishing . . .

Nardi stood still and tried to understand.

Brigitte stood still and tried to understand.

Brigitte started to run around the arena.

Nardi fell to his knees and buried his face in his hands.

The immobility of the magus.

The hundreds of eyes.

Nardi and Brigitte: the hour runs and hits . . .

Brigitte and Nardi: the hour runs and hits . . .

Giant moments with the whole silence in the world gathered under a circus tent.

Nardi sitting on the edge of the arena and mechanically repeating: Brigitte, Brigitte . . .

Brigitte slapping Garuda and shrieking: give him back!

The giant roar of laughter swelling the walls of the giant tent.

Nardi felt his salty tears as he saw Brigitte struggle in Garuda's arms. The magus laughs. The children laugh and clap and stomp.

The two old people desperately feel like running towards each other. Embracing.

They meet again, though, with the dignity of the knight and princess separated by the crusade.

The two old people leave the arena. Cheered. Tightly holding hands. As if facing death.

***

At home, in the evening, relishing the vine-leaf rolls, drenched in fresh cream, with spicy Arab sausages and peasant bread, draining it all in a rough Merlot, ruby sparkles in the crystal glasses, listening to *Queen*, treating their souls to *Made in Heaven*, alone, yet not at all lonely, the old couple looked like they had forgotten all about the circus and the vanishing. They smiled to one another secretly and occasionally cast a look at the TV to see if their beloved *Seinfeld* was already on.

At one point, Brigitte told Nardi:

'The hour runs and hits . . . time is forever.'

'It was just like a fairy-tale . . .' Nardi whispered.

And suddenly they saw themselves in a tense embrace by the side of the arena. The audience on one side, and on the other the magician, the circus manager, the tamers holding their dogs and leopards on leash, the torch jugglers, the wire walkers and trapeze acrobats, the horse-riders walking their steeds, the clowns on single-wheel cycles, in the inside arena circle and in the circle outside it, all looking for them everywhere, talking feverishly, gesticulating.

And the two playful old people holding one another on the edge of the arena, between the two worlds, the inner one and the outer one, perhaps one and the same life, really, it all depends on how you choose to look at it, but the old couple, Nardi and Brigitte had stuck their roots deep in the edge of that circle, the only magical circle, where any vanishing is possible, and they were looking playfully, curiously, and knowingly at the funny madness of the world, thinking that life is an endless and extraordinary tale of tales which they would be telling to their children, their grandchildren, and not just them, thinking to bring on their island and into their house on the edge of the circle a small and cheerful puppy, a loud fox-terrier, named Ara, such that their own tale should always start like this:

"Once upon a time there were an old man and an old woman who had a zany puppy called Ara . . . "

A TALE ABOUT CHILDREN

Ever since he gave his wealth over to the poor, ever since he had become a monk early in his life and up until his last day as a bishop in Myra, Lycia, Saint Nicholas had been a kind and simple man.

One night, after having roamed the harbor of Myra and lent a strong helping hand to the fishermen and sailors, oblivious of his aging white beard; after having comforted the pains of the needy; after having offered food and fairy tales to the children who flocked around him calling him 'Father Nicholas', the old monk was resting on a rock besieged by the waves. He had fixed his eyes on the starlit tapestry of the night and was breathing in the salty breeze of the sea.

Beside him sat his downy-bearded disciple, who had followed the old man for a year now in all his pilgrimages. He was looking at the Holy Writ that Nicholas would never part from and that his thin hands with bony fingers now pressed against his pointed knees.

Father Nicholas felt his inner struggle and gently urged:

'Tell me. Go on, tell me what's burdening your soul.'

The disciple fidgeted awkwardly and finally braced up:

'Father Nicholas, I've not been able to find the answer to a question that has been troubling me for a while now. Here I am, learning and learning from you, from your books, from the other elders, from the people . . . And you can't say I haven't been giving it my best shot . . . But . . .'

'Well, go on . . .'

'Well, you know, the Lord said unto Thomas, 'I am the way, the truth, and the life: no man cometh unto the Father, but by me . . .'

'So?'

'So, I still can't find my way!'

Father Nicholas laughed gently:

'My child, this is the written Word of God, but it is not meant to be read in its letter. You have to read it such that you may live it with your heart and your spirit. Then you will find the way . . . and all the rest. But you have to be very patient.'

The disciple fell silent. Then he picked a pebble and threw it far away, as if meaning to break the wave that was drawing close to the rock.

'But, Father', he burst out, 'you have told me this so many times . . . Sometimes it feels like I am getting a sense of it, but many times I believe it's not very clear in your mind either . . . Forgive me, Father.'

Father Nicholas put his arm around his shoulders and started a story:

'Listen, my child. All my life I have been fond of children.

Now, in my old age, I am praying every day that God may grant me the gift of being able to bring a smile on each child's face. I toil day and night to do just that, and I await His sign.'

The disciple turned and looked at his tall forehead, his bright and meek eyes. He found there a quaint mixture of mirth and sadness, which made him quickly ask:

'Father, is it true that you, who are a saint for us, have not yet received a sign?'

Father Nicholas tapped him lightly on the shoulders and reassured him:

'No, I haven't. But I will.'

'When?'

'I don't know . . . when I am a child again.'

THE TALE OF A BEAR AND A FOX

Once upon a time, there lived a man whom God ordained to be strong, wise, and lonely like a bear.

This man lived his life to the fullest, feared, respected, and heeded by the people, but without too many friends.

His bear-like gifts helped him withstand all trouble, relish in tranquillity his victories and pleasures. Though powerful, he was not cruel. Though wise, he was not conceited. Though lonely, he was not a grumpy hermit. The people were never really dissatisfied with him. On the contrary, they valued him and treasured his presence. They needed him. More and more every day.

Naturally, before long he became one of the most feared, respected, and heeded leaders in a world that could not easily be conceived without him.

Until, one day, something happened to him that resembled the well-known story of the bear and the fox. In a deep forest, after a long and harsh winter, the bear

came out of his den as the grass was beginning to sprout. Spring brought everything back to life and the bear – the Heavy Lord of the Land and the Forests – was quite hungry. He even felt angry as his stomach began to rumble. Then he made a list and started to stalk the woods. He met the rabbit and told him: 'Here: see? You're on my list, I have to eat you up.' The rabbit saw himself on the list, saw that the bear was right, and the Heavy Lord ate him up. The same fate befell the deer and the wolf. Then the Heavy Lord finally met the fox. And although the fox had fooled him and his fathers before him, he was so hungry and so determined and so confident, that he showed the fox his list. The fox looked at the list and this time went for no trick, but simply said:

'Bear, I understand you. But couldn't you just cross me out of that list? Please try.'

The Heavy Lord of the Land and the Forests shook his big head and asked shortly:

'How?'

'Just like that.'

And the bear crossed the fox out. Just like that . . . Then he went on his way, looking for the other entries on his long list.

This is what happened one day to the bear-like man.

And he finally realized what gift God had bestowed on him, and asked God that he could turn into a simple human being. Before it was too late and he would have to remain a bear for the rest of his days.

And some say that God took pity on him.

THE TALE OF A JOURNALIST

The origins of the journalist go back to the dark Middle Ages.

Some say that this what amounts to practically a new humanoid species was the town crier, the news bearer, or the drummer of the hamlet. According to other folk sources, it was the medicine woman, or the gossip gammer, the priestess of the village, or even, anonymous sources claim, the Unholy himself.

Well, bearing this in mind, sometime around the end of the twentieth century a journalist of undisputed world prestige decided to write a shocking story that would open the eyes of the world and change the destiny of the people, a story that would be the keystone of humanity before the Apocalypse, a story of legendary India.

Like a steed without spleen, the journalist roamed the libraries, the cultural centers, the tourist agencies, the embassies and the museums, visited scholars and diplomats, newspapers, magazines, and broadcasting corporations. In what was undoubtedly a record time, like the true and world-renowned professional he was, he managed to collect all the documentation together with the funding needed for a story of this scope. Indeed, many cautioned him that a country the size of a continent, with hundreds of thousands of people in it, a country known as the cradle of religions and philosophies, cannot really be understood or known, much less turned into a shocking and epoch-making story in just three weeks. But who can stop a journalist who has decided to reveal for the benefit of humanity another of those truths that gives any alert conscience the goose bumps?

Armed to his teeth, as a world-renowned journalist should be, with note pads, recorder, photo camera, video camera, and even some equipment procured directly from NASA, our journalist landed in New Delhi. As he walked out of the airport he was met by the guide and the driver, courtesy of the Indian government.

The journalist quickly dismissed the guide because he had no intention of being influenced by a government official. Then he got in the limousine (a British model) and with the unsophisticated, but nice and funny driver by his side, he set out to accomplish his life's story as he now called it.

Days went by like seconds and there was plenty for the journalist to record. He did his job like the true professional he was. Kumar, the driver, also offered invaluable help. He had a high-school education in the state system, as any struggling young man, his own life experience, and a few lines from the Mahabharata, which he had memorized as a child.

In temples, in tiger, elephant, exotic bird, snake, and crocodile reservations, in museums, on the streets, in bazaars, in universities, hospitals, orphanages, factories and restaurants, at the newspaper and television stations, practically everywhere Kumar was his guide, his translator, and, in a way, his friend.

The day before he had to return home, after the journalist had set for most of the working day his meticulously and professionally collected material in order,

more precisely just as he was telling himself that either he was going to get the Pulitzer or he was leaving his job, Kumar knocked on the hotel door.

'Sir', he politely started after the journalist had asked him to come in, sit in an armchair, drink some whiskey on the rocks with him for the forthcoming Pulitzer, 'Sir, when you first arrived here you told me you wished to wash your hands and face in the waters of Yamuna, the sacred river that runs through New Delhi. You also said you wished to dine with poor, unsophisticated Indians, like myself. To gain better, more direct insight, you said. I did not forget your wish. If you still have this wish, I am at your disposal, sir.'

The journalist quickly thought of his invitation to the American embassy cocktail, but being in a great disposition on account of the Pulitzer and of his mission as a journalist of world renown, he enthusiastically replied:

'Let's do it. You're an OK guy, Kumar. You'll have a place of honor in my story. Let's go.'

Kumar drove the British limousine across New Delhi. The journalist could review once more the temples, the buildings, the streets, the parks, the bazaars, the people, and India, this time as a connoisseur, he thought dryly.

***

Kumar stopped the car next to a railroad bridge, somewhere on the outskirts. They got out of the car and walked down the narrow path on the tall bank. The sun was setting and the horizon was lit as in the poems of Rabindranath Tagore, the journalist silently phrased it.

But he was interrupted by Kumar's invitation:

'Here, sir, you can take this path to reach the water.'

The journalist looked.

The dark and slow waters of the Yamuna ran filthy and oily. Garbage drifted on the lazy current. Not far from there, on a small island, some seagulls were pecking at a corpse.

From under his feet, as everywhere around, rose a heavy rotten stench.

Kumar tapped him lightly on the shoulder and silently invited him to walk the rather steep path to the Yamuna, the sacred river.

The journalist wanted to ask something, but he gave it up and walked heavily ahead.

He had barely taken a couple of steps when he stopped abruptly. His feet had sunk into something gooey, like a decomposing brown-green-yellowish sponge. In a flash, he realized he was walking on the back of a gigantic waste hill. He jumped back to his starting position, as if the place had burnt his feet. Back where Kumar stood smiling.

On their way back, in the limousine, discreetly sniffing at his clothes, the journalist felt he had to explain:

'Kumar, you must understand I am forever grateful for your help and friendship. But I'm afraid I won't be able to join your family for dinner. I would have absolutely loved to meet your wife and children, the whole family. I understand there's many of them and you're the only provider.

'I congratulate you. But you see, you must not feel offended . . . I have professional obligations, the protocol, the ethics of my profession call for me to go to this cocktail, which I really detest. You know, all these social events . . . But, honestly, my mind's hand touched the Yamuna', and his mind went *That must have knocked his socks off! I have to remember that "my mind's hand . . . "*

Kumar looked at him through the rearview mirror, his sincere smile exposing the pure white of his teeth, and replied in a friendly voice:

'Yes, sir.'

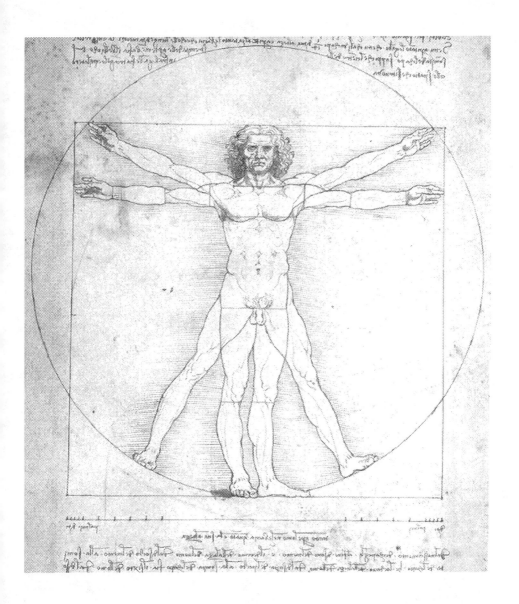

A TALE ABOUT LAZARUS

The multitudes were waiting on top of the hill that surrounded the cave.

Many from Jerusalem had come to Bethany, which was about fifteen furlongs off.

The sun was shooting flames, the hot air wavered, and out on the steps to the grave Jesus knew that many expect to be like the pillars of salt in this Sodom-and-Gomorra-like heat should they witness the miracle of a simple mortal being brought back from the dead.

Jesus knew that the resurrection of Jair's daughter or that of the son of the widow from Nain were nothing like this resurrection which was to be watched and judged by tens of Jews just before His entrance into Jerusalem.

He did not turn his head, He did not move towards those who surrounded and hungrily awaited to curse Him, throw stones at Him, kill Him.

The moment He told Mary: 'I am the resurrection, and the life: he that believeth in me, though he were dead, yet shall he live' and added in an almost commanding voice:

'And whosoever liveth and believeth in me shall never die', Jesus knew only too well that Lazarus' sister could only answer: 'I believe that thou art the Christ, the Son of God, which should come into the world.' And the witness bore by the gentle and humble woman was but the first sip of the cup to be drunk to the last.

He heard behind him the weeping of those dear unto Lazarus, He listened to the wailing of those frightened unto death, and He felt from all over the place the heavy, burning breath of the Prince of this world, He recognized the merciless and rebellious waiting, and He issued the curt, indomitable command: 'Get thee behind me, Satan!' which could only be heard by the heavenly Father. And He alone felt the air becoming fresh, the heat subsiding, the souls around Him raising their brow to receive Him fearlessly, joyfully.

Yet did Jesus know that the will of the Father was that the claw of Darkness should still tear at the soul and the flesh of each Jew, and that it should throw a tarry veil over each man's heart.

And Jesus groaned in His spirit.

But Lazarus had to be risen from the dead.

He smelled the black and toothless mouth of the grave put forth the stench of decay, of a man who had been dead four days, as Martha had told Him.

***

And Jesus groaned in Himself.

He heard behind him even His wretched disciples asking one another like people whose faith had gone astray: 'Could not this man, who opened the eyes of the blind, who had Jair's daughter and the son of the widow of Nain rise from the dead, have caused that even this man should not have died?'

***

And again Jesus groaned in His spirit.

He stood upright, raised His arms, with palms turned toward the grave, and lifted up His eyes. He looked at the heavenly Father and gave thanks in Words with meaning unto Himself: 'Father, I thank thee that thou hast heard me. And I knew that thou hearest me always: but because of the people which stand by I said *it*, that they may believe that thou hast sent me.'

And a light, gentle wind started to blow and his whole-piece linen cloth fluttered on His thin body like the touch of a gentle, white light.

And Jesus raised His voice to fill the heavens and the earth:

'Lazarus, come forth! Eleazar, whom God has helped! Come out, the Son of Man is calling for you!'

And Jesus once more drank of the cup that had to be drunk unto the last. And in a flash He saw Himself on the wooden cross, stripped, covered in blood, soiled, and crowned with thorns, a prey to the flesh which screamed its unbearable pain, a prey to the soul which shed blood tears for its body, a prey to His incarnation which no longer wished the terrible agony, so human, so like that of any man killed slowly and cynically, a prey to his hopelessness which made his vinegar-burnt lips move and utter: 'E'lo-i, E'lo-i, la'ma sabach-tha'ni? '

And he that was dead came forth, bound hand and foot with grave-clothes, and his face was bound about with a napkin.

'Welcome, Eleazar', Jesus murmured.

Like so many pillars of salt did the Jews look on Lazarus, that is, Eleazar, that is, 'God has helped'.

As if pierced by the sword of His Word, the disciples looked at the Christ as he stood motionless, arms stretched, palms turned toward the grave, his brow lifted toward Heaven.

And they saw a cross of gentle white light.

And Jesus watched Himself being brought down into the grave, bound hand and foot with grave-clothes, and his face was bound about with a napkin.

Then He said unto them:

'Loose him, and let him go.'

CHAPTER 7

If you live into Jesus the Christ,
sooner or later you will know the definition of Heaven,
the only true definition of Heaven:
"God is Heaven.
Not vice versa."
And, indeed you will find what a good smile means.
Like Jesus is smiling to you – right now . . .

(Theophil Magus)

THE TALE OF A HERMIT

There's a beginning and an end for all – or maybe not.

There are words to be spoken within us and without that all may rise and fall eternally in us and beyond us from the beginning of time – or maybe not.

And there's That Word in each of us – or maybe . . .

Once upon a time . . .

There lived a man towards the end of the twentieth century after Christ, somewhere (all right, wherever you wish). A middle-aged man. A man with family and children and all that, living like other billions of people in the human society entirely by laws, taxes, cars, computers, planes, visas, politicians, religious schisms, holidays, doctors, accountants, oil, meat, milk, and bread, in other words, a socially dependent man.

Yet our man, like so many others, like everyone else, practically, wished to become independent. At least a bit. Naturally, everyone tries as well as they can (according to their rank, their eye color, their bank account etc.).

***

Our man had learned about somebody's words – which had made that person famous and many think, o, how lucky some people are, you come up with a couple of clever words and next thing you know you're in all dictionaries and encyclopedias – words that have sunk deeply into his mind:

'The twentieth century will be religious or will not be at all.'

Well, unlike many, unlike countless others, our man really wanted to find out what in God's name those words meant.

O, do not expect that *X Files* or *Millennium* or the newspaper astrology columns, or the books on saints and magi, or the masses and round-tables of the clergy or other such things enlightened our man in any way.

But you have to admit that his was an honorable effort.

Finally, after a couple of years of searching, our man quietly bought a Bible and started reading. Quite industriously.

The reading took him a while.

He undertook it like extra-mural courses. Over several years, for there are obligations to one's family, to society, and you can't deal with the Bible without the aid of all kinds of dictionaries, and books, and commentaries, and it's like this book goes on for an eternity.

All went well and the dough of erudition was rising in our man. And, yes, yes, the world kept on turning as it should.

And every now and again, our man returned to the original thought, which he now called a 'meditation', to the words from where everything had started.

And, naturally, there came a day when he dropped everything and started thinking of God. Of course, this happened as soon as he learnt that the wonderful cake of erudition tasted moldy.

Gradually at first, then daily, thinking of God over and over again, our man finally started to pray, have wishes, ask himself questions, and supplicate.

And still his problem, the words from where everything had begun and which were the only ones he had not forgotten, was not solved.

At the dusk of his life he decided to leave his family, his grandchildren, his friends, society altogether, and set on a pilgrimage, as a modest tourist, naturally, hoping that maybe he was going to find the answer. It was all he asked for, no matter how good or bad that answer might be.

It goes without saying that by now he was speaking to God on a regular basis. Not as a bigot, naturally, or a sectarian, or a missionary, no, no. He spoke to God like a regular and slightly upset man.

His pilgrimage or planetary tourism, call it as you wish, finally proved useless.

But our man never stopped talking to God, not even after he eventually returned home, and when, no more than a couple of steps away from the end of his life, he realized – quite serenely, we have to grant him that – that some had forsaken him, some had forgotten him, and the family, well, the family rather pressed him to draw his will.

O yes, the day came when our man sitting all alone in his shabby, cell-like room spoke out in relative distress:

'Tell me, my Lord, please tell me!'

And after a stony silence, he heard something half-uttered and half-unuttered, within him and without, with no beginning and no end, and to be understood somewhat like this:

'But let Me speak, man! For once, let Me speak!'

And for the rest of his days, our man kept quiet and listened.

And he learnt.

More than he wished to learn.

THE TALE OF EDGAR ALLAN POE

The lonesome birds; they live for more than a hundred years; they easily learn human speech; they prove surprisingly intelligent; they express themselves rationally; and among the flying fowl there are some strange beings – the ravens.

I am over thirty and a loner. I have the qualities and flaws of an ordinary man. Possibly the only unique flaw or maybe a quality that distinguishes me from most of the rest, is loneliness. In different times I would have been a hermit in the woods. Yes, I have reached the age when I am convinced my only aim is loneliness. We all know that people are born alone and they die alone, but they hardly ever manage to live alone. Although it is alone that they believe themselves to be creative.

I'm in my armchair. I look out through the wide-open window. The sun lights the house in front of me and the buildings around.

The street is empty and it's hot. The metal whiz of cars coming from the avenue.

Children's voices in the school-yard.

I smoke nervously. My raven is gone. He took off three days ago. We had a frightful argument and I came this close to throwing an ashtray at him.

In the two years we've been inseparable friends we had many arguments over one and the same thing, but never have I become so enraged as three days ago.

I met him one day when I was lost in the woods just outside the city limits. He was perched on a branch and was scrutinizing me. He greeted me politely and offered to lead me back to the city. I was so confused and frightened that it all looked natural to me. I thanked him and he kindly showed me the way. As we parted, he said:

'Sir, you are not the first human I am assisting. But before I take my leave, I have to tell you that you are an idiot. In my long-lived solitude, I have noticed your kind shows quite a gift in this respect, yet you have reached the highest level of excellence. You are a charming idiot.'

I was stunned. The raven waited calmly. Finally, I exploded:

'How dare you! Explain!'

He slowly spread his wings.

'Wait, wait', I stopped him, 'tonight you will be my guest for dinner. We will talk and you will find I am no idiot.'

On his branch, the raven shifted his way from one leg to the other, pecked at his feathers, than crowed:

'All right, but you will not be able to prove the contrary. Any argument you may invoke, you will still be an idiot. A charming one, admittedly.'

He flapped his wings and clawed his wings on to my shoulder.

On the way back I couldn't refrain from trying to make him see that he was mistaken.

To start with, because, unlike him, I belonged to the only species endowed with reason . . .

No use.

The raven was unflinching in his conviction. I got upset and called him "a lousy parrot, a broken street organ", I cursed him, but to no avail.

The dinner went on beautifully. We chitchatted and the raven proved a consummate interlocutor. I fell for him, I asked him to stay over night. He accepted and thus we became inseparable friends.

***

And yet for the two years we have been together I was still an idiot to him. And often this meant a row, just as three days ago.

I miss him. His absence affects me deeply. *Where are you, dear friend . . . ?*

Two years in which, as the saying goes "a raven in need is a raven indeed", he was always there to offer the right advice, to share my joy as if he was my own soul . . .

But why should I be an idiot?

I am an idiot. I've been worrying pointlessly for three days. I reviewed step by step our friendship history, my only friendship in the world . . . No answer. None.

I put out my cigarette. I light another. The street is empty and it's hot. Too empty and too hot. My raven. My great secret.

I am a poor human being and what can exceed the beauty of compassion from a non-human soul to which you can confess without the doubts born of the love for any woman, child or man?

***

The street is empty. In front of me, the sun lights the buildings. The metal whiz of cars coming from the avenue. Children's voices in the school-yard . . .

***

Bang, I shut the window. I need a strong drink. I rise from my armchair. As I turn . . .

He is perched on a bookshelf. He leans his head to one side, opens his beak, and I hear his dry voice: NEVERMORE – IF.

I pick the ashtray and I throw it at him. He dodges effortlessly.

As he flies by, his wings caress me. Or do they? . . .

I close my eyes and hear the same dry voice: NEVERMORE – IF.

I open my eyes and watch him: he flies higher and vanishes – vanishes . . .

I spread my wings widely.

THE TALE OF THE LAST CONDOR

The last Californian condor stood on his cliff some thousands of feet high.

He was looking towards Los Angeles, frankly speaking, he was looking at Hollywood. His piercing look tore the horizon into rosy translucent mist.

The last condor saw his thoughts in the distance – pictures faded with time and with solitude.

And he thought that he too was a celebrity.

Maybe the giant bird ventured the only Californian superstar.

The last Californian condor spread his wings and glided on a gust of wind.

He drew a few wide circles around the cliff. And he closed his eyes pierced with the joy of smooth and boundless flying. Moments later, however, he remembered all the gossip and the tales about this joy, so he opened his eyes, and cut through the cold air to sit back on his cliff. Once more he looked towards Hollywood. Then he flew in a hurry to the plane that had followed him to offer protection.

***

The ornithologist showed up on the TV screen. He started talking about the governmental care for *gymnogyps californianus*. The tip of the condor wing pressed the smooth button. The picture was gone. And in his room, close to the Californian film studios, the last Californian condor snorted with discontent. The taped film was one huge lie. *What if I'm the only king in danger of becoming extinct?* He thought and decided to try once more.

***

For the third time that clear day, the *rara avis* took off to the cliff some thousand of feet high, and as he drew near his keen sight warned him of a very strange appearance.

Very strange, indeed.

The last Californian condor became restless. With each swing of his wings, with each fabulous swing, his restlessness grew. Soon the *Lord of the Skies* became dangerously nervous, a ruthless predator tense as a steel string. One could hear from afar the clamping of his large, crooked and still sharp beak.

From up high on the cliff the last Californian condor replied promptly with a similar clamping of his beak.

***

The air struggle was a five star performance, a super-show – unlike anything they have ever seen. The skies shook with the ovations coming from balloons, gliders, helicopters, vertical take off plains and from the amphitheaters carved in the side of the mountain.

***

The last Californian condor stood on his cliff some thousands of feet above the ocean. His piercing look was tearing the horizon – when sadness enveloped him.

Sweet and bitter.

Like the torn blood-red mist around him.

THE TALE OF THE KITTEN

This is how this tale has been told to the Buddhist monks for hundreds of years.

One beautiful summer day, the monks from the temple up in the mountains came all out to stack the hay on the meadow around the temple yard. It was a clear sunny day, a pleasant breeze was spreading the smell of hay and everybody was working with a feeling of clean and happy peace of soul. They all felt like children without any care. At one point, out of nowhere, a kitten showed up in their midst and started playing in the hay. It jumped, it gamboled, it ran in all directions, it scattered the hay with its little paws. One by one the monks stopped working to admire the enchanting grace and agility of the kitten. They seemed bewitched as they watched motionless the play of the animal. And the kitten went on jumping and gamboling mindless of the rapture of the humans.

After a while, the monks started one by one to play with the kitten. They jumped, they gamboled, and ran in all directions. Their happy juvenile laughter filled the forest. The kitten must have thought they were larger, slower kittens. For it was not afraid as it went on with its enchanting play.

All until one of the monks managed to catch the kitten and nestle it in his arms, caressing it and making it purr happily.

Then the row began. For each monk wanted the kitten for himself. Like as many children fighting over one toy.

Soon their angry voices were heard in the silence of the forest, in the peace of the temple.

The head monk reached the meadow just as the peaceful monks were on the brink of a scuffle.

The eldest monk told him what happened in a few words.

The head monk fell silent for a few moments that seemed endless like the unbounded clear sky.

Then he took the kitten in his arms, caressed it, and asked curtly:

'Who should have it, one of you, all of you, or the temple?'

The silence of each man's judgment was not long. The quarrel started afresh even more fiercely.

The head monk once more demanded:

'Decide!'

The monkish din was the only answer.

Than the head monk commanded them:
'Watch!'
And he tore the kitten in half.

***

When the pet novice of the head monk returned from his long pilgrimage, he was immediately brought to the head monk's cell.

Inside, having fasted and meditated for many days, the head monk met him affectionately and invited him to sit by his side. Then slowly and dispassionately he told him what had happened.

Then he asked:

'What would you have done in my place?'

The novice stood up, went to the threshold, paused for a moment looking his teacher in the eye, then picked up his sandals full of the dust and mire of the many roads. Slowly he placed them on the top of his head. Then he left the cell without a word.

***

For hundreds of years the Buddhist monks have sought the hidden meaning of this tale. Especially that for any true Buddhist, it is a well known fact, and even more so for a Buddhist monk, that the killing of any living creature is a crime and loving everything around them is a sacred duty.

For hundreds of years the Buddhist monks have sought the hidden meaning of this tale for it is said that the moment the sandals full of the dust and mire of wandering stood on the shaved head, both the teacher and the novice reached their illumination.

And for hundreds of years the monks have provided thousands of answers and interpretations for this tale.

Possibly all true.

***

But the wheel of destiny keeps turning and none but the One, the Lord knows what the year, the day, the hour, or the instant may bring.

***

One beautiful summer day, the monks from the temple up in the mountains came all out to stack the hay on the meadow around the temple yard. The sun, the clear sky, the pleasant breeze, the smell of hay . . .

And the kitten, like quick silver.

And the tale was spun as before, a long, long time ago.

Except that now the head monk was the one-time novice.

The monks surrounded him.

They each remembered what had happened once with the kitten.

And they each waited: for the death of the kitten or the unraveling of the hidden meaning.

The head monk caressed the kitten, nestled in his arms and spoke:

'The sun is shining. The sky is clear. The breeze is spreading the smell of hay. The birds fly in the air and never wonder about the air. The fish swim and never wonder about the water. The hay must be stacked. Let the kitten be. Everything is so quiet and peaceful.'

Then he let the kitten go. And the little animal started to jump and gambol and run in all directions.

And the monks stacked the hay with the souls and hearts of children without a care.

Indeed, they say less than an hour later they have forgotten the kitten that played freely.

Everything was quiet and peaceful.

A TALE ABOUT GOD

Once upon a time there was an old man.

A hermit.

His life had unraveled for years in a more or less known place, somewhere in the mountains.

Many claimed, laymen, priests and monks alike, that the old hermit was a saint.

And the hermit had once been given a novice, whom he had raised from his early years as a father would.

And the novice believed that the old hermit was a saint.

And one day he asked:

'Father, how may I find God?'

The hermit sighed.

Then he shook his head.

Finally he smiled kindly.

But he did not answer.

'Help me, father', the novice urged him. 'How ? Through smell, through taste, through sight, through touch, through hearing, through thought, tell me how?'

The old man called him and had him sit by his side.

He stroked his head, he smiled again, he sighed again, then he slowly, but firmly spoke:

'If you smell Him, He is like a breeze; if you taste Him, He is like a taste; if you see Him, He is like an apparition; if you touch Him, He is like a touch; if you hear Him, He is like a sound; if you think of Him, He is like a thought; if you can do all of these together at the same time, then *He is no longer.*'

'Then . . .', the novice mumbled horrified, 'then – He . . . is not?!'

'O, Jesus', the hermit laughed lightly, without remonstrance.

After a while, with a crystal clear and profound voice, like an old bell's call of a monastery from the high mountains, he said:

'My son, *God is that, is Who . . . He is.*'

Then he fell quiet and together they listened to the silence.

***

And as if speaking out of the silence the old man added:

'**God is in God** . . .

Keep searching.

With your heart . . . keep searching, my son.'

CHAPTER 8

That was the true Light, which gives light
to every man that cometh into the world.
He was in the world, and the world was made by Him,
and the world knew Him not.
He came unto his own, and His own received Him not.
But as many as received Him, to them gave
He power to become the sons of God,
[even] to them that believe in His name:
Who were born, not of blood, nor of the will of the flesh,
nor of the will of man, but of God.
And the Word was made flesh, and dwelt among us, and we beheld his glory,
the glory as of the only begotten of the Father, full of grace and truth.

(John 1/ 9-14)

A TALE OF NEW ORLEANS

It is well past midday in New Orleans.

The milky blue, almost translucent boundless sky reflects the heat from the blinding distant sun. Everything seems steeped in a gigantic steam bath: that's New Orleans at this time of day. Stoned from the scorching heat.

And yet, through some hourly miracle, Jackson Square lives restlessly turning each moment into a froth of busy days. In front of Saint Louis Cathedral, simple, white, and slender, and at the entrance to the oasis that looks as if it were painted by Douanier Rousseau in a fit of solar delirium – the park beckons you to meditate before or after the prayer, everywhere as in a magical live puzzle – clowns, mimes, musicians, actors, Tarot card readers, crystal fortune-tellers, bards and troubadours, painters, Fellini's dream world nurtured and adored by the Americans, the Europeans, the Asians, the Africans, the ceaseless flow of tourists. Jackson Square is Babel resurrected and the hot air vibrates with the blues, the jazz, the Louisiana ballads, revived every now and then by the hooting and bell-ringing of the steam boats licensed to float on the old and yet undefeated, giant Mississippi.

Soaked in their sweat and as if walking on sand, Andrei and Brigitte are crossing Jackson Square and heading for the park entrance.

They are taking their time. They look around and their eyes sparkle with delight. This circus is life itself forever changing, forever extinguished and revived. And these two can never miss that, since each of them is a healer and a magus of life. Andrei is a poet. Brigitte is a doctor. He is Charlot's double, yet more of a dreamer and also tough guy. He's got the same kind, compassionate smile, though. She is an Aztec reincarnation and her slender body, tall forehead, slanted bright brown eyes, the genuine joy springing from this apparently fragile creature, all make you think of a good fairy.

It's as clear as day that they couldn't but be in Jackson Square.

They walk slowly side by side and the tourists take them to be the brother and sister of the infant clowns, musicians, painters, actors, crystal fortune-tellers.

The cameras flash like brief lightening.

They were both born in Transylvania, one is American, the other is German. Andrei looks around and thinks of his last book,

Hail Babylon! He meditates on the story *Radio Messiah* soon to be devoured by Broadway.

Brigitte looks around and thinks of sick men and sicknesses, always the same and always different, no matter where or when. The magic circus of Jackson Square reflects their thoughts without a quiver. They both think: *Life without hope is absurd.*

And they both see the Angel at the same time. White and winged, eyes like burning coal, standing with a faded glow on a pedestal at the gate of the garden painted by Douanier Rousseau.

Andrei says in Romanian:

'This is the first time in twelve years I've seen an angel here . . .'

They both step closer and drop a few coins in the simple cardboard box by the pedestal.

The Angel thanks them with a slight nod and a faint flutter.

Andrei and Brigitte each wave vaguely and walk to the garden gate.

Andrei sees his grandmother teaching him *Our Father.*

And as in a cathedral of his heart and soul, he hears himself, deep inside: *What if I am Saint Andrew, the first apostle called upon . . . to heal . . . poetry? . . .*

Brigitte sees herself dressed in her doctor's white coat, stethoscope hanging from her neck, in a big, brightly lit room full of nice toys. She's surrounded by children aged three to five laughing heartily as they try to sing along, and she thinks: *What if I am Saint Brigitte, protector of . . . life . . . and healers?*

***

Andrei and Brigitte stop at the gate of naïve Douanier Rousseau's garden. They slowly turn to face the one already asking:

'What if I am the Angel?'

The crystal words envelop them like a breeze.

The place is getting cooler.

The Angel nods slightly and flutters its wings faintly, prompting them to walk past the gate.

And Andrei tells Brigitte in English:

'This happened in Jackson Square. It's not the heat, it's just life.'

'Zim-zaladim bam-baaa . . .', Brigitte tries to reply and fails.

She bursts into laughter.

They both laugh.

The Angel also laughs.

THE TALE OF THE IMPOSSIBLE OASIS

(. . . *dedicated to my Master* Vladimir Colin)

He looked like a spirit or ghost, the way he paced around the hospital ward. His steps slow and light, dressed in his white gown that went all the way down to his ankles, and bathed in the light of dawn that sparkled in the snow on the outside window ledge. Still slender, broad-shouldered, and upright, the old bard ran his agile pianist fingers over his tall vaulted forehead, straightening a rebellious lock of his dark-copper mane. Behind the thick glasses, his azure eyes gazed on the depths of his soul.

The old bard sucked avidly from his cigarette, then turned to his only disciple who sat quietly on a chair by the hospital bed.

The old bard was the last in a long line of bards from the "Land of Vam", a direct descendent of Vam, he who had faced and vanquished forever the pagan gods through his loving sacrifice. The old bard had written and spread across the wide world the *Legends from the Land of Vam*. But in his long agonizing wandering on this earth he had also set on paper many other diamond words, for the enjoyment of all human beings, for what else, if not joy born of pain and tears and love, are *The Fairy-tales, Dwarf Tales, The Tales of Man, The Invisible Fish, Pentagram, Time with Horseman and Raven*, and the many songs about the perishable man and his non-perishable soul, since they are all made in praise of our Lord.

Thus the old bard reviewed himself and a smile blossomed like a snowdrop in the corner of his mouth, burnt by fever and tobacco . . . As in a flash of memory of the earth, he saw tens of little children's faces from all the people of the world lit with the joy of his fantasies with dwarfs, giants, fairies, Princes Charming and beautiful damsels, witches and dragons, magic animals, forests and castles, wise grandfathers, and many more. Then he saw his elfish Marcela, merry as a ball of life in perennial spring, cuddling in his arms or using her magic brush to turn his fantasies into immortal images. He saw once more his wife passing away with a smile as if chiding him with infinite love: *Don't you be doing anything silly and don't be long. I've so many more fairy-tales to bring to life. I'll be waiting, don't be long . . .*

The old bard felt like crying, but he looked around and braced up when he saw the hospital bed, the hospital table, the hospital lamp, the hospital plate and cutlery, the bed pot, the bed flowers and the traces left by the people of the hospital world, living on a hospital planet at the end of the second millennium. He clenched his jaws, he shivered, and his heart shrunk.

But he did not cry.

The old bard heard deep inside something like the whisper of a brook, he heard the words of Jesus: "If you continue in my word, then are you my disciples indeed; And you shall know the truth, and the truth shall make you free."

The old bard asked himself if the truth had set him free and if he had anything else to confess: *To whom shall I confess and how and what?* he raised his prayer.

He looked kindly at his only disciple, who had watched and looked after him for days on end, as if he had lived all his life on that hospital chair, by that hospital bed, thoughtful, awkward, hurt, and furious with himself for not being able to defeat death, "which is but another birth and another joy", the old bard would have liked to tell him, but he never could, not before, and not now as he stood in front of him like a spirit or a ghost.

'Listen carefully', he told his disciple. 'It's really much easier and much better, trust me, to give you a piece of my soul, rather than confuse your soul with the words of this world. So listen:

"He had been surrounded by the dead for some time.

Nothing on the outside showed them to be dead, they looked just the way he remembered them, and they behaved as before when they used to go to work, or wait for their pension, or attend someone's funeral, or go by their business, rejoicing, fretting, getting bored, but Ilarion knew exactly when each of them had died."'

The old bard stopped talking long enough for him to light another cigarette, *the last*, he thought, and his disciple looked like he were made of alabaster and he were a wandering Jew.

'I'm still alive. Listen:

"When they started beating the drums, we all gathered in the square", Ilarion said, "because if we hadn't gone there on our own, they would have made us do it. The sky was blue-black, a sore sight, and in the old days we would have tried to heal it, but now everyone was counting their bruises and could not be bothered to think of other pains. Shut within ourselves, we were waiting in the square, and the muzzles of the weapons held by the figures in black uniforms were grinning, ready to spit darkness at us.

The commandant gestured and the drums were quiet.

'Your land is ours', he reminded us standing up on the tip of his tall boots then swinging back on his heels, he always did that when he summoned us, he would swing as he talked to us, his hands joined behind, and the motion of his rocking body somehow came across to us forcing us to listen to his words, which otherwise would have been lost, shut within ourselves as we were, 'from now on you will have to pay if you want to walk this land, and as our laws are fair, those with only one leg will only pay half the tax, and those crippled of both legs, will only pay a quarter for the license to touch the land with their crutches.'

There was a rapping of drums, the commandant turned his back on us, and we went home.

And since we had long been without money, we started crawling on our bellies."

The disciple quickly recited like a schoolboy dying to be praised by his teacher:

'*The Impossible Oasis. The Dead* and *The Last Phase*. Published in 1984 by . . .'

'Enough. What are you doing, what are you saying?' the old bard interrupted.

'But . . .'

'Enough. Listen: "Down with art, down with the artists! Long live the humanists!" But also: "Cultivate your mind and you won't be left behind. The illiterate litter less."

In the hospital ward, a spirit or ghost, bathed in the light of dawn that sparkled in the snow on the outside window ledge, dressed in his white gown that went all the way down to his ankles, the old bard laughed so hard he felt his belly was going to split.

The disciple alone sat on the hospital chair and, lost in his solitude, he gazed at the body of the last bard of the Vam tribe, lying on his back on the hospital bed. Inside, the disciple was endlessly repeating the old man's last words.

'I leave you *The Impossible Oasis*. To have and to hold, to love in truth, for as long as you and your heart shall wish.'

Seeing him like that, the old bard, a spirit or ghost, came to his side and tapped him on his shoulder:

'For God's sake, why can't you understand already? "Cultivate your mind and you won't be left behind. The illiterate litter less." Answer me now, for how long do you and your heart want it?'

Misty-eyed, the disciple laughed:

'Forever.'

A TALE ABOUT CROWS

"Consider the ravens, for they neither sow nor reap, which have neither storehouse nor barn; and God feeds them. Of how much more value are you than the birds? And which of you by worrying can add one cubit to his stature?" (Luke 12/24-25)

The crow sat on a branch in front of her young (lined up on another branch), strong, obedient, ready to take in their mother's last lesson before they took off to their new life.

The crow crowed tenderly, yet authoritatively:

'My darlings, this is the last lesson I'm ever going to teach you. I beg you, listen carefully, I will not say this twice, after all, this is the crow's creed in the world.'

The young crows crowed, flapped their wings affirmatively, full of respect for their mother.

'Well', the mother crow started, 'you have to know you are a special breed of fowl. And this is all due to your special bond with the humans.

For if it weren't for us crows, man would have never invented the Scarecrow. That is, the pathetic stuffed dummy humans think we are so scared of.

Nonsense! You know very well how silly this is to us.'

The young crows crowed merrily.

'But we are special birds', the mother crow went on, 'because humans have lived and will always live by our side, as we do by theirs. Wicked humans claim that we are filthy crows and birds of ill omen, hopeless thieves, that we flock together in fall and in winter to foretell bad weather, epidemics, harsh winters, that we vanish in spring, that we destroy the crops in summer, and other such preposterous, idiotic stuff. We are to them so different and ugly, that when they get bored they hunt us for sport. In short, they take us to be the scourge of their lives and a punishment for humanity, and the age-old proof for this is the Scarecrow. Are you with me?'

The young crows hopped a couple of times on their branch, signaling they had no problem following the argument.

'Well', the mother crow raised her voice, 'here is the genuine attitude of crows towards man:

In spring, when the earth turns green and teems with new life, when all shines bright and we are all revived, man starts fretting: he plows, he sows, he mends, he builds, he trims, he cleans, he waters, he freshens, he multiplies, he keeps accounts, in a word he toils all day and falls flat with exhaustion in the evening. While the crow sits on a branch and looks, rather famished and faint from the long winter, and just goes: *hmm* . . .

'Then, in summer, when man tends the crops, prepares the harvesting, defends himself from the dry season, the raging rains and the furious floods, when he continues his spring work, and counts and keeps accounts, and fills the land with his Scarecrows, and comes back home exhausted in the evening and gets so drunk that he falls flat in a ditch only to start over with the hangover in the morning, then what does the crow do?

'Why, the crow sits fat and satisfied on a branch and looks and just goes: *hmm* . . .

'The fall comes and there is human havoc. Man goes desperate. He harvests. He picks. He fills his granaries. He crams his larder. He squeezes the juice out of the grapes. He prepares the wine barrels. He gathers the potatoes, the corn, the apples and pears. He stitches and mends. He gathers wood. And much more.

Weddings, baptisms, funerals. He worries about the winter and he grunts by the brandy pot, he gets drunk and he sings, that is he yells at the top of his voice, and he occasionally beats up his wife, 'cause the winter is no laughing matter . . . And the crow? As always in the fall: chubby, shiny-feathered, belching with satisfaction and looking over the shoulder at the humans and just going: *hmm* . . .

'Finally the winter. Snow, blizzards, ice. Frost and frost bites. Men slaughter swine. They sit and warm themselves. They taste the fruits of a year's toil. They drink plum brandy or hot wine with cinnamon, they smack their lips happily and tell tales until they fall asleep by the hot oven and start snoring. In the morning they drink away their hangover with sauerkraut juice or a shot of chilled plum brandy, then they feed the fowl and the cattle, frown at the cluster of crows, and go inside to warm themselves. Either there or in a pub, they engage in heated discussions about the Christmas and especially about the coming year, for look at those damned crows, crowing of ill omen, God damn them!

'And what does the crow do? Nothing. It just sits on its branch cold and hungry. It looks at the snow-clad houses and streets, at the coiling smoke coming from the chimneys and just goes: *hmm* . . .

'There it is, my darlings. A rather lengthy lesson, but the last, which I believe pretty much covers everything there is to say about this.'

The young crows, which had been producing muffled grunts, now started laughing out loud.

Not at all upset, the mother crow allowed them to hop on for a while on their branch, flapping their wings and jeering. Then she motioned them down to silence and uttered in a clear and firm voice:

'Enough of this laughter ! Take wing and the Lord will protect you. But heed this last lesson and study it patiently on your own. So that you may never be afraid, not even of the stuffed, ragged horror of the humans . . .'

'The Scarecrow', crowed the young crows.

QUIDAM'S TALE

Quidam was born like all babies are born. His father saw him a few days later and exclaimed: 'Ah!'. Then he slapped his hips lightly and said: 'Ah'. Quidam grew up with full maternal, paternal, and social attention. A normal child, then. And welcomed. Benefiting from a sufficient amount of determination, like a child whose education had been serious and unexaggerated, Quidam's life ran un-abruptly, unswerving, and uneventful, on an almost ideal slanted plane, through all forms of education from the primary school to the college for productive engineers, so that by the end of his childhood-adolescence-youth, he had become an indispensable member of society. A normal citizen, then. And all who knew him closely or remotely could only say: 'O, how wonderful!'

On their death bed, his parents whispered in agony and with tenderness, the perfumed air vibrating with their parental satisfaction: 'Quidam . . .' Their daughter-in-law caressed her beloved Quidam with her bland, slightly opaque look at each of their demises. And she kissed him, wept as expected, then moderately blew her nose.

Quidam was thirty-eight when his first child was born, whom, quite naturally, he named Quidam. A child who could only be good, and deserving of his parents' adoration, Quidam was. But the child was slightly different from the other children, for it was a boy-girl. Nevertheless, despite his father's moderate meditation, the conclusion was: we, his parents, know that this is nobody's fault, and even if we are to suffer all our lives, our sufferance should be without futile exaggerations, as expected. Quidam junior was raised like a normal boy-girl. And having earned a degree in economy, he-she became an excellent accountant. But before that:

Once, in the midst of Quidam junior's puberty, after Quidam and his wife had had the expected amount of wine, they agreed that they are among the few citizens to have a boy and a girl at the same time. All night they repeated those fine words and from then on, their peace of mind was indestructible. And Quidam had another child, a girl-boy. Although his peace of mind was indestructible, Quidam shed a tear. But nature decreed that Quidam shed more tears, containing his normal feelings of normal happiness, for this child only lived ten months. The parents incinerated the small body. They placed the small amount of ashes in an aluminum urn, which they set in their window case, quite naturally, between a China ballerina and a China dog.

Quidam and his family lived in a modern social environment, a productive city. The wealth resulted from the industriousness of the inhabitants meant ideal conditions for a long normal life. Quidam's townsmen lived an absolutely balanced life. They were friendly within the bounds of common sense. They always greeted one another in the street. They only loved animals that yielded fur, feathers, food, fertilizers, soap. They mixed business with pleasure. They never engaged in futile conversation or action. And they always greeted one another in the street.

One day, happily returned from work, as he always did, having finished his lunch and satisfied as always by his wife's wisdom in designing the menu, Quidam entered Quidam junior's room. And he felt just like a balloon ready to blow up. He looked around in amazement. Then he gently stroked Quidam junior's head, who was peacefully asleep. Again he looked around in amazement. And he felt just like a balloon ready to blow up. 'Well', he whispered careful not to disturb his offspring. Then he went for a walk. In the city park where he again felt abnormally attacked, that is, just like a balloon ready to blow up. That night, sleeping in his bed, he tossed slightly.

Years passed. Quidam had long forgotten all about it. But one day, as he came into his room, he felt just like a balloon ready to blow up. He immediately summoned his wife and told her what he was experiencing. She pondered for a couple of seconds and replied firmly: 'You're bloated.' And he went: 'Oh, I must be constipated'. Quidam junior who was in the room added: 'Let's find an adequate tea'. For three days Quidam only drank tea and ate toast. He lost weight, true, but he declared he felt excellent. 'It's only normal, dear', his wife said.

Five more years passed since the horrible sensation in Quidam's moderately built torso. *Time and a normal life pour concrete over unusual sensations.* Quidam had once again forgotten all about it.

One perfectly normal day (meanwhile Quidam junior had married, as was to be expected of any normal boy-girl), while visiting the young couple and discussing the necessity of normal life all over the world, Quidam realized with abnormal surprise that his fingers were clenched on the arm of his armchair. His cheeks were all flushed, and he felt his ears slightly flutter. He stammered faintly, then all of a sudden he said: '. . . ba-balloon ready to-to blow up'.

Quidam junior didn't quite understand, but he nodded and confirmed: 'Yes, yes, an obsolete world'.

Quidam looked around.

The following day, at work, Quidam looked around. The third day, in the park, Quidam looked around. Out in the street, Quidam had started to look around. In his dreams, Quidam was looking around.

Then, one perfectly normal day someone asked him:

'Why are you looking so afraid around you?'

'Do you think so', Quidam replied. 'My eyes may be inflamed.'

'The flu?'

'I don't really know', Quidam mumbled, 'but I'll make sure it won't happen again and I'll be on the look-out for the flu.'

And the following days he started to look normal again.

Seven years later, one perfectly normal day, Quidam, like any other citizens, was dying. Quidam junior could barely hear his father wheeze: 'a ba-balloon just a-bout . . .', and the rest he couldn't make out. Then there was silence.

Quidam had exploded.

A TALE ABOUT MOSES

(. . . dedicated to my Saint Teacher Nicolae Steinhardt)

There are many unknown and mysterious tales of Man and his Making on earth.

In the writings of the Essenes, the Dead Sea Scrolls of the Qumran caves, there is also this story:

" . . . And Moses went up from the plains of Moab unto the mountain of Nebo, to the top of Pisgah, that *is* over against Jericho. And the LORD showed him all the land of Gilead, unto Dan, and all Naphtali, and the land of Ephraim, and Manasseh, and all the land of Judah, unto the utmost sea, and the south, and the plain of the valley of Jericho, the city of palm trees, unto Zoar.

And Moses looked at the land from dawn to blood-red dusk. He stood tall and straight as the cedar trees of Lebanon, though he was 120 years of age.

And the sacred rod he held in his fist not for support, but rather as a scepter.

His alone, Moses, God's chosen.

The sunset was putting off the horizons when Moses called God.

God came and stood before Moses as He had before, when He talked to Moses like a friend.

Moses mumbled something then sat on the rough rock, placed the rod by his side, coughed a few times and finally spoke:

'Here I am, Lord, forty years a priest and a prince, forty years a priest and a shepherd, forty years a priest and a provider of statutes. Believe me, Lord, I am grown sick of the days, of the lack of understanding of the statutes, sick of this stubborn people . . . I don't know anymore . . . I just don't know . . .'

The Lord enveloped him with kindness.

And saw his hardened face, cheeks like the two tables of stone where His finger had written the commandments upon Mount Sinai.

And Moses looked tired and hardened.

'Moses, Moses,' said the Lord.

Moses sighed:

'Lord, you have shown me Your glory. You took me by Your side, on Your rock. And, Lord, I have studied and spread Your Law. Lord, this stubborn people shall know now and forever, as all peoples of this earth, that You are the One and holy God. But I don't think I can or want to suffer their lawlessness and sins . . . of which You, Lord, are so aware . . .'

'Moses, Moses,' sighed the Lord.

'Well, there it is, Lord: I no longer want to cross the Jordan. Lord Almighty, I ask of you to seize me unto you, take me to you like you did Enoch, or in whichever fashion You may wish, but don't leave me among them. You know this only too well, Lord, they will rebel, and they will forget, and they will sin, and they will once more divide their soul for the score of gods born by their minds which are the slaves of the flesh and the lust and the faithlessness and the vanity . . .'

'Enough, speak no more, Moses!' the Lord commanded.

Moses did not start. Instead, he replied firmly:

'And yet I love them, Lord. And I pity them so much.'

The Lord wrapped him once more, very carefully. And suddenly He started laughing loud:

'Moses, Moses, you look like a sour old bear. Moses, when did I ever see you laugh, in beauty and purity of soul, from your heart, after the fashion of My own heart? Never, Moses.'

Moses darkened. The line between his eyebrows deepened. The glow in his face grew dull. He shrugged and mumbled:

'Lord, even my song was a curse . . .'

'Moses', the Lord said, 'I am that I am. And the Word is the Law and the Grace, could it be that you have forgotten that? Listen carefully: I will leave you here for forty days. If you find Me in your prayers such that you may laugh with all your good and gentle heart, then Moses will I take you to Me. Seek and you shall find.'

The Lord left Moses alone. The top of the mountain disappeared in the blinding light in the middle of the night.

And in a red cloud during the day.

***

The people were trembling in their camp, beating the dust with their foreheads in front of the Tent of the Covenant and waiting for Joshua to take them across the Jordan. And oath after oath rose from their mouths, from their yearning after the Promised Land and from their fear of the punishment they had suffered to help them remember.

From the top of the mountain, Moses saw and heard all that, and remembered what had been once, and saw what was to come. And he could not find a reason to smile, let alone to laugh. And he seemed to sink deeper and deeper in a mortifying sadness.

But on the last day, when he had reached the bottom of his suffering, and he looked like a shadow of light from all the fasting and praying, he asked the Lord to forgive him.

And suddenly Moses could see, or hear, or feel no more. It was as if all has ceased to be. Yet it was not the abyss. Then gradually and ever so gently everything cleared up. Like a gift of infinite joy towards love and forgiveness, the Child was born of the Word of infinite light. And seeing Him, Moses rejoiced with all his heart, with all his soul, with his entire mind, and with all the might of his being.

And the Child smiled to him, and Moses laughed from the beauty and purity of his heart."

THERE ARE NEVER ENOUGH STORIES

by *Liviu Antonesei*

The Advantages of Slow Reading

I received by chance the text of the present *book* written in a program which my computer does not have. For the people who know about it, the script was written in Times Ro and I read it in Times New Roman. Consequently, because I neither had the program nor the time to get a hold of it, I read the script slowly and painstakingly, because I was supposed to replace the Romanian diacritics by some weird graphic signs. Luckily for me, they were the same for each special Romanian character. So, I was happy because of the constancy of the rule of substitution.

Apparently, no effort is useless, every effort is rewarded.

Usually, I am a fast reader, sometimes I even read in a hurry. In this particular situation, I was forced to engage in a slow reading, I took my time to study the text, I paid more attention to nuances, details, to the structure of the stories, to the characters' replies. In a nutshell, I was more careful about the text itself, I read the text more attentively, underneath the mere perception of the material text. This is what I suggest to all readers of the book TRILOGY of THEOPHIL MAGUS – *The Truth.*

Of course, I could ask the publishing house to edit the text in Times Ro and print it in Times New Roman, but unfortunately this is such an unusual demand. Furthermore, it would mean imposing my will on the reader, doubting his ability to read slowly, but efficiently, making pauses, coming back, self-suspending and re-starting. As far as I am concerned, I am not so suspicious about the reader, I consider her/him to be the writer's "brother" or "accomplice" rather than his enemy.

In this book, Leonard Oprea seems to be one of the remarkably few writers capable of creating, in an authentic manner, such a relationship of brotherhood, of complicity with his readers. A surprisingly large number of readers, I may say. My suspicion subsides, however, when I think that these numerous and very different potential readers each have an individual perception and manner of reading, ranging from what critics call, "the basic", "the innocent" reading to a very refined one, which enables true archaeological expeditions towards the multidimensional layers of the texts by this author who was born in Brasov, Transylvania's capital, took a long detour through

Bucharest, and now seems to have settled down in Boston, though nothing is definitive with him.

A lack of topographic settling matched by a happy lack of cultural and artistic settling.

Few of those who are familiar with Leonard Oprea's science fiction style from the beginning of his writing career or who remember his civic militancy could foresee the countenance of his writing today.

In his prose, the discerning eye may detect the traces of Borges, Mrozec (especially the short stories) and Malamud, but these traces are so discreet, so diluted, so naturally assimilated, so thoroughly internalized, that they do not affect his originality of vision and writing. Why? For the simple fact that may strike some of us as a paradox that his originality comes from an appeal to *originarity*, an immersion into the cultural abyss of the species. Leonard Oprea's fiction today is lodged in a larger intertext that spans the entire text of the Bible and the Talmud, the Arabic, Tibetan, and Zen-Buddhist teachings, Christian and pre-Christian folklore, Hinduism, the life and work of Edgar Allan Poe and Andrei Codrescu, that of his friends, and even his own life and that of his family. In fact, we are dealing with a "democracy of culture", though different from the natural one proposed by another Romanian writer and dissident, Mircea Dinescu. It is truly sensational the way in which in *Our Story*, for example, the writer seems to listen to, read, and re-write his own life, one whose story is told by another One, the absolute alter ego, the divinity that is one, although it has so many names. I am equally struck by the fact that this polymorphic originarity is coherent, almost organic, and it does not give even for a moment any sensation of artificiality, of incongruity. Is it because "mythologies" are frequented in a distinct fashion in each story? Maybe, but I believe there may be a deeper, more fundamental reason: beyond the culturally marked, and therefore historical, originarities, there is a genuine originarity, that pre-dates history, that I would even dare call "pre-Babel-ian", if this term, too, were not marked culturally, bearing history's fingerprint.

***

Two, even three types of reading

I have already said that Leonard Oprea's stories can be submitted to an infinite number of readings. If I were to attempt some sort of didactic ordering, I would say they are placed on a scale between two extreme, "pure" types. First of all, we have the genuinely innocent reading, that comes in one of two fashions, either believing that the "tales" are taken as such from their cultural space, without any modification, or, on the contrary, taking the stories to be made up by the author and to be the result of his individual labor. Though not very accurate, such readings are not necessarily unwarranted. After all, this is how "the larger public" reads important writers such as Homer or Shakespeare, Eminescu or Dostoievski. And there is an undeniable pleasure of such "pure reading" that I also crave, although it became impossible for me and for those like me whose taste has been altered by the "criticism of pure reading".

And thus we enter the territory of the second type of extreme reading, the one marked by the cultural experience of the reader who has lost her/his innocence, a reader who cannot help noticing that the "tales" are neither produced entirely by Leonard Oprea, nor "borrowed" by him from their original cultural domain, from the bulk of historically marked motifs. In fact, beyond the excellent writing Oprea displays in this volume, his great talent lies in his ability to metamorphose motifs, in his smooth playing with terms, a kind of *la modification* which has nothing in common with the technique used by *le nouveau roman français* (the French New Novel), though I am at a loss finding a better term for it. *La modification* confers originality to the present prose and has an impact not only on the "mythological" reasons, but also on the "biographical" ones, whether we are talking about biographemes, as much as I have access to them, or about the context graphemes, whether we are in "1 May" Market in Bucharest, in New Orleans seen through Andrei Codrescu's eyes, in Leonard Oprea's native Brasov or anywhere else in the visible world of the author. Slow reading allowed me to try a multitude of exciting exercises of detecting biographic-literary clues, deluding myself that I have discovered a lot of carefully locked "secrets". This is an additional pleasure that not many readers can afford, of course, but whose absence does not affect in any way the pleasure of reading in itself, either "innocent" or "refined".

***

Stories ? Never enough!

I believe that the title above states the essential about Leonard Oprea's work. He really is responsible for a genuine and quite intense delight of reading. I do not know if the author himself enjoys writing, though I tend to believe he does, but he definitely offers his readers an immense pleasure. First, because he is impeccable when he "carves" the "originary material". Second, because he has the gift of telling stories, and he does it in an admirable way. The return to the pleasure of telling stories, to the art of the tale, may very well be his chief narrative device. This does not mean that, when in need, he cannot appeal to updated technical innovations, as in the case of the already mentioned *"Our Story"*. But the technique assists the story, it never substitutes it, as so many modern or, *horrible dictu,* postmodern writers would have it. Of course, Oprea's greater ambition may very well be to simply tell the story exquisitely not through excess, rather through parsimony of literary devices.

Indeed, I wonder whether in *"Our Story"* and in other such texts, his intention was not to exhibit how he can visibly renounce certain techniques, in order to recapture the actual story without which true fiction cannot survive. It is as if he was telling us: "Look at how well I have mastered composition techniques, look at my consummate craft, no less than that of any good writer, but notice the difference: I can freely give up this arsenal, because I have rediscovered a long lost gift, I can still tell stories, my own stories". Yes, he knows how to tell his stories and all the tales of the world because he uses *la modification* to place his unmistakable fingerprint on each of them. In this, *no doubt that Leonard Oprea is a genius "thief" who strangely wants to enlarge not diminish the public domain he furtively relishes.*

The TRILOGY of THEOPHIL MAGUS – *The Truth* contains *40 Tales about Man* "taken from the world and given back to it". Alas, not enough of them. There is no such thing as too many stories, they are never fulfilling enough. Another advantage of slow reading, which I cannot refrain from recommending to every reader once again, no matter how "innocent" or "refined" they may be, is that you can "make the reading take longer" and tell yourself it may never end. You could read one or two tales a day, in the manner that stories are told in the evening, before going to bed. Of course, if Leonard Oprea did like Scheherazade when confronted with a mortal danger, he could help us make the reading of his delightful tales take longer. But does the author really have a choice? Isn't the life of every storyteller in danger since her/his life depends on the capacity of "telling" more stories. I can imagine Leonard Oprea on top of a mountain, fishing for motifs in the nearby oceans, throwing back the smaller "fish" and keeping only the big ones, preparing for us the awaited stories (that the better of us really deserve) to take us to the end of the world. Here I am, trying to capture the tone of my good and far-away friend's fiction. I don't know if I got it right, but, as a character in a famous American novel says, "at least I tried".

And if Leonard Oprea willingly assumes Scheherazade's fate, I promise that I will try again. During the slow reading of this book, but also while I was writing the afterword, I repeatedly asked myself if one can say about a writer who is still alive, whom I had the privilege of knowing, that *he is a very good writer, even a great one.* I have always had my doubts about it *until now* when I braced up and concluded that *you can.*

In a nutshell, all important writers were alive once and in most of the cases, their value was recognized, at least by some of their contemporaries who even knew them directly.

***

(*Liviu Antonesei* – poet, novelist, essayist / Iasi, Romania, 2008)

THE END